F

A Thornton Brothers Time Travel Romance Novel

Book 3

Cynthia Luhrs

This book is a work of fiction. Names, characters, places, and incidents either are products of the author's imagination or are used fictitiously.

First Knight, A Thornton Brothers Time Travel Romance Novel

Copyright © 2016 by Cynthia Luhrs

All rights reserved, including the right to reproduce this book or portions thereof in any form whatsoever.

Acknowledgments

Thanks to my fabulous editor, Arran at Editing720 and Kendra at Typos Be Gone.

Chapter One

England—Present Day

Jennifer Wilson sat up, leaned forward, and let out a gasp, leaving a ghostly imprint of what looked like a dragon on the clean window.

"Everything all right, miss?" The driver glanced at her in the rearview mirror, waiting until she nodded before turning his attention back to the road.

"It's... Wow. Have you ever had a serious case of déjà vu? When I looked at pictures online, this place looked familiar, but the feeling wasn't nearly as strong as it is now." Finger pressed against the glass, she traced the outline of the castle ruins. "Being here, so close...it's as if I've come home. Isn't that silly?"

He pursed his lips. "Not at all. Somerforth Castle has

stood guard over these lands since the twelfth century, and was rumored to have been a Roman stronghold for several years. Who knows what kind of energy emanates from an old place such as this? Or perhaps it's something deeper, given to us from the collective consciousness when we're born."

She blinked at him. "A philosopher and a driver?"

The man looked to be in his early fifties, with salt-and-pepper hair and a strong jaw. Warm brown eyes met her gaze.

"I read a lot. Maybe you had an ancestor who worked at the castle or you yourself lived here in another life."

"It would explain the feeling, that's for sure." Jennifer inhaled. "I didn't see the ocean on the way, but I swear I smell it."

"Aye. If we kept going you'd catch sight of the North Sea. One of the last earls sold off an immense portion of the lands to cover the taxes owed. Somerforth used to stretch all the way to the coast. There's an old legend about a great white shark that has lived in the sea for centuries stalking unwary victims." He chuckled. "Likely the old curmudgeon didn't want anyone traipsing about on his lands."

"I'll make sure to stay out of the water." The castle was situated on the west coast close to the border of Scotland. They'd passed through Newcastle, where they'd stopped so she could get out and stretch for a few minutes. Otherwise it had been nothing but small villages and lots and lots of green. Her mother would have been miserable. She adored the energy of a city and all the excitement that went along with it. Not to mention more people meant better hunting grounds for her next husband. Marriage. What a crock.

The black sedan rolled to a stop. Before Jennifer could open the door, the driver was there, helping her out.

"I'll fetch your bags."

"Thank you," she called out as he disappeared around the car. After sitting so long—first the drive to the airport in Baltimore, then the flight, and then another car ride from London all the way to the ends of the country—her backside ached. Cracking noises filled the soft spring air when she stretched to work out the kinks.

The driver placed the bag on the ground. Reaching in her purse to pay, he waved her away. "Already taken care of. Enjoy your summer."

"You too," she said, but he was already gone, leaving her standing in a field looking around and wondering where to go. Thanks to her dad for taking care of the plane ticket and car ride and to her mom for supplementing her spending money.

An actual ruined castle. Her fingers twitched, itching to pick up a paintbrush and capture the contrast of the verdant rolling hills against the formidable gray stone fortress. With a little imagination, she could picture

Somerforth Castle as it must have been in its glory.

"Oi, you going to stand there with your mouth hanging open all day?" A scruffy-looking guy, wearing faded jeans with holes in both knees and a navy t-shirt proclaiming *You had me at BACON*, stood there grinning at her.

"You must be the Yank."

She nodded, but before she could answer, he was off, striding across the insanely green landscape. So much better than the concrete, metal, and glass of Baltimore.

"Thought so. We had another Yank here a while back. She looked like Barbie come to life, but she was wicked good with a knife."

"I... That is, my name's..."

He went on, talking over her, not bothering to look back and check if she was keeping up or not. "Don't know what happened to her. Thought we'd hear how she was getting on; guess she's been busy. You Yanks are always running around with fifty things to do and never enough time to get them all done. Never stop to take a breath. She came here to train." The guy waved a hand around his head. "I hear you're here for the dig." He stopped, and Jennifer was so busy looking at the surroundings that she almost ran into his back.

"You don't look like an archeology student."

"More like a long-term student. Or at least I was." She arched a brow. "What exactly does an archeology student look like?"

He ignored the warning in her voice as he looked her up and down. "You've got the bland, low-maintenance look going for you. Kind of like a shy vampire girl with that hair." He scratched his nose and shrugged, seeming to give up on trying to categorize her. "I'd say you look like a head-in-the-clouds kind of girl, not a dig-in-the-dirt chick." Then he leaned in close. "Fancy a drink after you're settled in?"

"Maybe when elephants fly. How about you show me where I'm supposed to be and I'll take it from there?"

"Yes, ma'am." He saluted and turned on his heel.

"Don't mind Charlie. He annoys everyone." A woman with short, spiky brown hair and a tattoo of a dragon circling her neck and ending at her bicep held out a hand. "I'm Mary. Welcome."

"Jennifer. Nice to meet you."

"The professor and his students went into town to pick up supplies and should be back soon. He said you'd be here today. In the meantime, I'll show you around."

The guy with the bacon shirt had left without a peep. Jennifer was sure he was harmless, and she hoped everyone else would be friendly, because if it were up to her, she'd hole up in her room and read all night. Too many people and too much interaction exhausted her, sucking the energy out of her, as if she'd run a marathon and then gone dancing all night.

"Great. Are you part of the team?"

"No. I'm with the re-enactment group. None of us are

allowed to camp inside the ruins, it isn't safe, so we're on the edge of the woods, and the students are a bit further down."

That explained the medieval-looking clothing. As they walked, an old truck caught Jennifer's eye. "I don't think I've ever seen so many stickers on one vehicle."

Mary patted the truck. "It used to be a pumpkin color until Charlie started covering it with pithy sayings. Who knows where he found them all. Now I don't even notice."

"I like the one that says *jammy*. Kind of looks like the stickers are holding the truck together."

Mary laughed, and Jennifer had the feeling she'd made her first friend in England. It was a good feeling to find someone you could talk with. Usually it was difficult for her to make friends. She much preferred to be the one curled up in a chair in the corner, nose in a book.

"You're probably right about the stickers. I try not to think about it too much, especially when we're going over bridges." Mary widened her eyes. "Bridges make me nervous. Always have."

Jennifer's guide kept up a stream of chatter as she led her around the encampment. The ruins were situated to take advantage of the landscape, allowing the inhabitants to see who was approaching from any direction . The sky was so blue that she could almost imagine she was underwater, walking around the lakebed looking up at the surface of the water instead of the sky.

In this area of camp the history buffs wore medieval clothing, and many were fighting with swords or shooting arrows at targets set up in a grassy field. The white tents were a stark contrast to the colorful landscape.

There weren't many women, a few scattered about working on various projects. Their dresses looked to be wool, with cotton shirts or dresses underneath. How on earth did they stay cool all summer?

"Over here is the professor's camp. Easy to tell the difference, since the tents are all blue." Mary took her through the ordered rows until they came to a tent set slightly apart and a bit crooked, as if it had been hastily erected before the person ran off to do something more interesting.

"Is that the dig site?" Jennifer looked across the field at the hole in the ground, trying to sneak a peek under the tarp when the breeze lifted up one edge and a scent drifted out. She inhaled. Roses. But there weren't any she could see.

"Do you smell roses?"

Mary twitched. "Roses grow in the old garden, but we're too far away to smell them."

"Like the ocean."

"I'm not much of a swimmer, but some of the guys go for a dip once in a while. It's a bit of a hike, or a short drive if you take the truck."

As Jennifer sniffed again, a sound filled the air. Bagpipes. She looked around to locate the source, but didn't see anyone. Scanned the tents and grounds, but there was one there either. Someone playing music?

"I don't believe it. The piper plays for you." Mary's eyes were huge as she took a step back. "The woman who was here before, he played for her too. Interesting."

Others had stopped what they were doing, heads tilted to the sky. Some stood, mouths open in surprise, and a few wiped their eyes.

"What a nice welcome. Who's the musician?"

Mary eyed her up and down. "What did you say your last name was?"

Chapter Two

England—June 1334

"Do not listen to women. Nefarious schemers, the lot of them."

Edward cuffed his brother on the shoulder. "What happened with your betrothed this time?"

Christian re-sheathed his sword and stomped over to a stone bench, where he sank down, scowling.

Legs stretched out in front of him, Edward watched his brother's men practice their swordplay in the lists.

"There is a rumor about me amongst the lasses. None will have me because of it."

"Surely you jest? Winterforth is not as large as Somerforth, and you are puny but have gold, title, and lands aplenty. What wench wouldn't wish to plight her troth with you?"

At a score and four, his brother was the youngest of the Thorntons. Yet he should have been long married with babes of his own.

Christian let out a weary sigh. "If you tell John or cousin William, I will never speak to you again."

Edward held up his hands. "I will keep your confidence. What could be so bad? Do you snore loud enough to wake the dead, or pass wind of such stench the lasses run away?" Then, seeing the utter dejection on Christian's face, Edward turned serious. "I give you my word: I will not speak of whatever you say."

"All because of one night." Christian leaned closer to Edward. "At court last year, a wealthy widow took me to her bed." He snorted. "The lasses always flock to my bed, and I had heard she did not want to marry only to enjoy the bed sport, so I eagerly followed her to her chamber."

Edward tapped his foot, trying to hide his impatience.

"I was deep in my cups and I... Bloody hell. I fell asleep. The next morn, she told all I suffered grave injury as a boy and could not have babes." He threw up his hands and paced. "None will have me. Each lass finds a reason why she cannot marry me, or their sires agree to the betrothal and the girl runs away. They would rather be beaten than face a life without children. I will die alone."

"You are Lord Winterforth," Edward said. "Not as handsome as I, and your swordplay is lacking, but you are a Thornton, and any would give much to ally with us. Marry a girl and put a babe in her belly that will end the rumors."

His brother shook his head, a look of anguish on his face. "Nay, Edward. The last one ran away to France to marry a baker rather than face me at the altar. I am doomed to loneliness."

Edward rolled his eyes. "Then put a babe in one of the serving wenches' bellies, give her a few coins, and stop this nonsense being spouted amongst the eligible maidens of the realm." Edward threw up his hands. "Hell, marry a foreign lass."

Christian looked horrified. "I will have an English bride, and I cannot put a babe in a woman's belly on purpose. Father taught us to cherish all women. Not to ill-use them. A babe would be my responsibility. What do I know of raising a babe? 'Tis women's work." His shoulders slumped. "I cannot."

"Ask Charlotte or Anna. All of the women in our family enjoy meddling. Surely they can find you a wife who will not bolt before you have bedded her."

"And you? Why then have you not married if 'tis so simple any dolt can do it?"

"I have been visiting eligible maidens, and soon I will choose one to become the lady of Somerforth."

Christian raised a brow.

"Harrumph. None have suited me thus far. All of them are much too biddable."

"I would gladly have a meek and quiet wife. One who will leave me to hunt."

Edward cuffed Christian. "Dolt. Do not let Melinda hear you say such, or she will swear to find you a shrew to plague you the rest of your days."

"You want a future girl? Now who is daft? There are none to be had. 'Tis not possible."

Edward sighed, knowing his brother was right. "Mayhap. I would be content with a lass who looks me in the eye and speaks her mind."

Christian snorted. "You'd have better luck finding a faerie."

The next morn, Edward embraced his brother in the courtyard. "I vow to find us wives."

"Methinks I should visit the abbey and make a large donation. The nuns will pray for us."

"Aye. One accepts aid wherever it is given."

'Twas a pleasant day as Edward rode to meet his captain and a handful of the men at an inn along the way. The journey to Somerforth would take three weeks if the weather held.

"Is Christian married?" Brom fondled a serving

wench as she brought ale to the table.

"Nay. The lad cannot keep his betrothed long enough to actually marry the girl."

"I say love them for the night, and in the morn move on."

Edward snorted. "Christian has wanted to marry and have a houseful of babes since he was a boy. I will find him a proper wife."

Brom looked unconvinced. "If I were to ever marry, I would ask Lucy or her sisters to find me a bride. Women know how to choose a bride, as men know how to choose good horseflesh."

"This is why you are unwed. Women frown upon being compared to horses."

"Do they?"

Two days from home, a rider met them on the road. "My lord." The man gasped. "A raid. We lost a great many sheep."

Edward swore. "Damned Armstrongs."

It had been almost a year since the Scots lost six hundred at the Battle of Halidon Hill while the English lost a mere fourteen. Since then, the raids over the border were becoming bolder and more frequent as hatred between the English and Scots grew. "Then we shall take them back and the rest of his livestock as well."

He expected the odd raid—'twas unavoidable living so close to Scotland—yet Gilbert Armstrong had plagued him for nigh on a year. Busy with other matters, Edward had not dealt with the man as swiftly as he should. Today he would take back what was his and more. Teach the arrogant whoreson a lesson he would not soon forget.

Chapter Three

Before Jennifer could answer Mary's odd question, a man skidded to a stop in front of them, kicking up dirt. He leaned over, hands on his knees. "You must be Jennifer Wilson. Is that a married name? Are you at all related to the Thorntons?"

Mary handed the intense man a bottle of water from a nearby cooler. "Jennifer, this is Guy. The man in charge of our merry band."

"Cheers." He guzzled half the bottle and wiped his face with his tunic.

"There aren't any Thorntons in our family," Jennifer said. "My mom's become a bit obsessed with genealogy thanks to her latest husband, and she's spent a lot of time researching the family. Thornton is a great name, strong and solid. I'd definitely have remembered it."

No one spoke again until the piper finished, the last notes floating away on the breeze.

"That was beautiful yet haunting."

"You just heard a ghost." Mary looked at Guy, and something passed between them.

"Somerforth belonged to Edward Thornton. The oldest of five brothers. According to the legend, a Thornton woman saved her people from certain death. We've only heard him play one other time, when Charlotte was here." Guy wiped his brow. "How about Merriweather? That name ring a bell?"

She shook her head. "Nope. Sorry." Then Jennifer looked around for anyone holding a cell phone. "Is this a welcome to England joke?"

Mary spoke up. "We never jest about the piper. His ghost supposedly haunts all of the Thornton castles. Only plays for the lady of the castle."

"I'd love to be a lady of a castle, but I'm plain, simple Jennifer Wilson. Sorry to disappoint you all."

The spell broken, people drifted back to what they were doing, though the sadness lingered in the air. She'd only been here a day and already she was daydreaming. Her parents would not be pleased. This was to be a summer where she decided the course of her life, not wiled the time away on fantasy and painting.

Guy looked at his watch. "The professor called. They're on the way. Be here in a jiffy. I'll see you around."

"Bye. And thanks for telling me the story."

Mary lifted the flap to the slightly skewed blue tent. Jennifer didn't care, as long as it didn't fall on her head. She'd never had much luck setting up a tent on her own.

"It isn't the height of luxury, but you'll be comfortable enough."

She peeked inside, pleasantly surprised. There was a tidy cot already made up with a pillow and blanket, a comfy-looking chair, and a tiny dresser.

"This is more than I expected." She looked over her shoulder at Mary. "Does everyone eat together? Something Guy said made me think not."

"No. We keep to ourselves most of the time. The students eat a lot of pizza, and we stick mainly to medieval dishes. You're welcome to join us one night."

The woman smelled of honey from the bread she baked. "I might just do that." Jennifer dropped the bag on the cot. She had the entire summer ahead of her. As she unpacked, the watercolors beckoned. The only decision was what to capture first: roses or ruins? Maybe she'd have time to paint after she met the professor. Surely he wouldn't expect her to start working on the first day?

A ruined castle. It was so romantic, with the crumbling stone, the smell of roses, and the invigorating scent of the ocean. Jennifer could picture a rugged knight riding out to protect his people, battling the bad guys and then coming home to her. He would look at her and no one else. No way would he want to trade her in for a younger model as the years passed. The scene playing out in her head was so vivid that she could smell the boiling oil and rotting garbage before it was flung over the wall at the enemy.

A quick search confirmed the expensive solar charger she'd ordered before she'd left was still there. Several weeks before the trip, she'd left a pair of sunglasses and bag of groceries behind, all on the same day. Ever since, she'd gotten a bit paranoid about forgetting things, and now double-or triple-checked her bags. Talk about OCD. The fancy charger was for the e-reader and the phone—not that Jennifer planned to call anyone; the phone was mostly for music.

When she arrived, she'd texted her parents to let them know, and told them she'd try to check in once every few weeks or so. Her mom replied saying she'd send an email when she and hubby got home from their cruise. Fine by her. Both of her parents liked drama in their lives, and the constant upheaval of arguments between their current spouses and each other, then making up, wore her out. Seemed like someone was always mad at one of their friends. It was exhausting just hearing about it. Who wanted to expend so much negative energy? Nope. Give her peace and quiet. No drama, thank you very much. Jennifer planned to paint and read whenever she had downtime this summer. Nina Simone sang about the other woman while she finished unpacking.

"Hello? Jenny?"

A man appeared in the opening of the tent, casting a shadow over the small space.

"I'm Jennifer. Professor VanHemert?"

The man took a step back as she came out, blinking in the sunlight. Best guess put him in his early sixties. He had a full head of silver hair and a perpetual tan from working outside most of his life. Lively brown eyes behind a pair of wire-rimmed glasses took her measure.

"Lovely to meet you. Glad to have you with us for the summer. How's your father getting on?"

"He's fine. He and the new wife had a baby about six months ago. They're spending the summer traveling to the last twenty states they haven't seen yet."

"Good, good. And your mother? You have her eyes, you know."

Jennifer sighed. "She and Shane are off for a month-long cruise."

The professor blinked at her. "Shane? I thought..."

Between clenched teeth, she said, "Shane is the new husband. They married seven months ago." Heat traveled up her chest to settle in her cheeks. "Her fourth, not that anyone's counting," she muttered. "Thanks again for taking me on."

"Of course. I always enjoyed your parents at university. Though they were a fiery mix even then."

Chapter Four

Edward shifted on his horse, his foul temper making him snarl at the men. “Bloody Gilbert Armstrong. The man has no honor.”

“’Twas a good day—none were injured. He cannot say the same.” Brom’s nose had been broken again, but other than that, Edward’s captain was unscathed.

Almost home. The scene below on the rocky beach made Edward briefly close his eyes. Alas, when he opened them, ’twas still there.

“Is aught amiss, my lord?”

He pointed. “Shipwreck.”

Grimly, Brom nodded. “We needs see if any survived.”

The closer they came to the water, the less Edward spoke. Not since the horror of his twelfth summer had he gone into the sea. That day haunted him still. The wind tormented him, making him hear screams he knew were not there.

One of his men reined in his horse. "All are dead. French, by the looks of them. The men are gathering up what has not been ruined by the sea." The man rubbed his hands together. "We found jewels and gold. And a great many casks of wine."

Brom smiled wide. "We will drink our fill tonight."

Edward forced his voice not to waver. He was no mewling babe—he was a warrior feared across the lands. "The sea is a vengeful mistress. Bring the dead. We will give them a Christian burial in the cemetery in the wood."

"'Tis a fine day. Mayhap a swim?" Brom spoke in a low voice so only Edward would hear. The last vestiges of the horrors were banished to the light as Edward clapped his friend on the back.

"Not this day, Brom."

The horses, sensing they were close to home, picked up the pace. The men jested amongst themselves, boasting of how much wine they would consume and how many wenches they would bed this eve.

The skirmishes between the Armstrongs and some of the other, lesser clans across the border were becoming more frequent. There was much unrest across the land. Edward would post additional guards on the walls.

"You could end the fighting with Armstrong. His

daughter is of age, and I saw her watching you. She is beautiful."

Edward grimaced. "While I am not opposed to taking a Scot to wife, she is not the one for me."

"And what, pray tell, is amiss with this wench?"

"The lass is afeared of her own shadow. Her father beats her." He scratched his ear. "And yet I would always be on guard. Would she poison me at supper or stab me with her dirk while I slept?"

"Rather difficult for a man to beget an heir if he is always sleeping with one eye open." Brom chuckled. "You require a good woman. All of your brothers, save Christian, have married. As eldest, you should be chasing after your son's children by now."

"A future girl would make a good wife. My brothers are pleased with their brides."

"Not this again. No matter how far you travel, you will never travel far enough to find one of these women."

Brom had been with Edward since they were small boys. Edward was six years older, and one day had found the boy being pelted with mud by a group of older boys. After Edward tossed each one into the cesspit, he took Brom under his wing, taught him how to fight, and they had been inseparable ever since.

His captain had saved him on several occasions during battle, and while he had offered to raise the man's station, Brom was content guarding his lord's back.

Now he snorted. “Don’t be daft. You would be better served kneeling in front of a faerie hill and calling for one to come out. There are many eligible maidens who would be happy to spend your gold and give you children. Do not waste your life waiting for something you can never have.”

“Harrumph.” While he would admit Brom was right, Edward still looked everywhere they went, hoping he might notice a woman who looked out of place. Or in peril. For each time his brothers found their future girls, the women had appeared out of nowhere. Edward knew he’d spooked his men on several occasions by staring into the fields and woods around Somerforth. Some had begun crossing themselves, fearful of faeries hiding in the trees. He would have to take care. Perchance his captain was right. ’Twas time to take a wife and stop waiting for one who might never appear.

Chapter Five

The professor led the way to the dig, pointing out the current area they were excavating.

"This used to be the garrison. Somerforth was not only an immense fortress but also considered quite modern for its time. When the first Earl of Somerforth built the castle from stone, a cache of mosaics, remarkably undamaged, was uncovered as the workers were digging. Likely left over from Roman occupation and left behind, forgotten for time until the thrifty earl put them to use on the floors. Pity we've only found a small section. They are quite beautiful."

"I can't wait to see them." Jennifer pointed to a piece of equipment. "I was picturing something more primitive, like the shovels and brushes over there. There's so much high-tech equipment."

The professor chuckled. “Have to keep up with the times. We have several generous donors, which allows us to acquire the latest technology.” As he knelt down to retie the end of the tarp, he said, “I’m afraid you may be rather bored. With eight graduate students, it’s mainly a gopher job. Fetching tools and driving to the village to pick up mail, supplies, and lunch. That sort of thing. Also a bit of sending emails and taking pictures. There will be plenty of time with nothing much to do. I do hope you can entertain yourself. What is it you do again, write?”

“I paint.”

“Excellent. You’ll find plenty of inspiration.” The professor stood, his white shirt and khaki pants looking a bit rumpled. He was short and compact. Solid. She liked solid. Dependable.

“Need me to start this afternoon?”

“No, no.” He waved her away, already preoccupied. “Tomorrow morning is fine. Dinner will be served at seven tonight. A woman from the village brings the meal, and another comes to make breakfast, which is served promptly at six. So you only have to fetch lunch. Usually sandwiches, pizza, fish and chips, or meat pies from the pub. We start working around seven.”

“Perfect,” she said as he meandered away, talking to himself and making notes on a small spiral pad he’d produced from the pocket of his khakis.

The rest of the afternoon was hers to do as she

pleased. Jennifer grabbed a bottle of water along with the canvas bag containing her paints, and decided to capture the castle ruins. Tomorrow she'd set up in the old rose garden. To thank the professor for making room for her this summer and keeping her parents from driving her crazy with their "you need a good job or find a rich man and get married" speeches, she'd do a watercolor of the ruins, one of the coast, and another of everyone digging.

With no job upon graduation and the prospect of taking a mercy job working for her dad at his doctor's office, Jennifer was grateful he'd taken pity on her. Though in truth she thought he was afraid of her mother's temper, and that was what motivated him. Didn't matter to her—a gig was a gig. Her dad had friends at the local college and had pulled some strings. Jennifer didn't care if she cleaned or ran errands; it didn't matter. For the entire summer she was living in the English countryside, sleeping next to a ruined castle. So much better than working retail or being stuck in an office all day.

When she returned home at the end of summer, she'd buckle down and find a job. Maybe at a college or museum doing whatever they needed. But for now, living in a tent in Northern England, almost on the border of Scotland, was her idea of heaven on earth.

The afternoon light deepened into evening when Jennifer stretched and went to work cleaning her brushes. Standing back to view her work, she closed her eyes then opened them to see what her gaze went to first. What needed more work or stood out too much. She'd set up at the furthest point of the castle. The dig was taking place at the rear, and she was looking at what would have been the front.

She pulled the rough sketch out and shook her head. Before starting the painting, an image had come to her as fully formed as if she were looking at it in real life. The sketch showed Somerforth as she imagined it. Not a ruin but a fully functioning castle. Her hand moved of its own volition as she frantically captured the picture in her mind's eye before it vanished. When complete, Jennifer let out a breath. It had felt like someone else was moving her hand, for she couldn't possibly have created such detail from her imagination.

Tonight at dinner, she'd ask if anyone knew what Somerforth looked like before it fell. For as much as she'd searched online, Jennifer couldn't find a single image, other than the ruins and one sketch of the front, which looked nothing like what she had done. The professor might like both works, even if one was only a product of her fanciful imagination. For now, she tucked the sketch into the back of the pad and followed a worn path back to the camp, stopping on the way by a picturesque bubbling brook to wash up.

When she sat down at the outdoor table that evening, one of the grad students, a pretty girl with golden hair, sneered and whispered something to her friend. Why did there always have to be a mean girl in the bunch?

"Don't mind Monica. She's mad you got the open position instead of her bestie this summer." A guy with hazel eyes nudged her. "I'm Mark."

She introduced herself to those she hadn't already met and tried to ignore Monica. Dinner was stew with bread so delicious Jennifer could have eaten an entire loaf. Mary had a magic touch. Mark said she made it with honey, which reinforced her suspicions when she'd met the woman, and explained the smell that followed Mary everywhere she went. Exhaustion set in as Jennifer sipped a pint, the buzz of conversation lulling her into a stupor. The time change and travel had finally caught up to her.

"I'm about to fall asleep. See you all in the morning."

"Need a wake-up call?" Mark looked hopeful. He was really good-looking, but she'd already heard how he'd dated every single girl at the site and in the village. Absolutely not the guy for her.

"I've got an alarm on my phone. Thanks anyway."

Back in her tent, she climbed into the narrow cot with a sigh of relief. Too tired to read, she lay there, letting her body relax. The faint sound of bagpipes drifted in on the breeze.

"Sorry to disappoint you, but I'm not a Thornton," Jennifer whispered as she blew out the candle.

Chapter Six

As the mill on the estate came into view, Edward heard a scream.

"Brom. You and two of the men with me; send the rest home."

A woman came running toward them, and he galloped to her. She was wringing her hands and weeping, so he could not understand her words.

"Mistress, cease your weeping. Tell me what is amiss."

She took a few breaths and blew her nose on her sleeve. "My boy. He was on the wheel when he slipped and fell in. He cannot swim and there is no sign of him. I fear he is drowned."

His skin clammy, he was finding it difficult to draw breath. Everything seemed brighter and louder as he slid off his horse.

Brom put a hand on his arm. A look passed between them. "'Tis hot this day. Shall I go in after the lad, my lord?"

Relieved, Edward nodded. "As you will."

His captain quickly stripped off his clothes and dove in as Edward stood on the bank wringing his hands like the woman next to him. At least he wasn't weeping.

Brom broke the surface, took a breath, and dove under once more. Edward touched the woman's arm. "Calm yourself, madam. We will find your boy."

Two heads appeared. Brom held the lad in his arms as he swam to the bank, and tossed the child to Edward. The child was pale and unmoving. No, it could not be. He rolled the boy to his side, roughly pounding him on the back until the lad retched up water. He opened his eyes, gasping and coughing up more water until he was exhausted from his efforts.

The woman fell to her knees. "Thanks be to you both. You saved my son. May the Lord bless you and keep you."

The miller ran to the woman, dusting his hands off on his pants. "What's happened?" He saw the boy and fell to his knees, holding him close. "What have I told you about sitting on the wheel when you cannot swim?"

"Forgive me, Da."

Edward watched the man's emotions as he pulled his only son to him, and something deep within shuddered and broke. He wanted sons of his own. Lads he would be proud of. Knights bearing his name through the centuries, Somerforth filled with laughter and family. All this time he had been waiting for a woman who did not exist. Not for him. 'Twas time to marry and forget this future-girl foolishness. He was a dolt.

A girl carrying a covered basket came over the hill, touching her hair.

"Is John dead?" She peered at him. "He cannot swim, yet he sits on the wheel." She kicked at her brother. "Fool."

"My daughter, my lord."

The girl made a small curtsy as she blushed and looked at her feet. Edward could not have said what color her eyes were, nor if her face were pleasing, as she never looked up at him.

Mayhap Brom had it right: he needed a biddable girl to take for a wife. "Do you like cherries?"

"Do you, my lord?"

"Aye, very much. They are now growing plump and ripe in the castle gardens."

"Then I do as well." She blushed again, shuffling her feet in the grass.

Edward rifled in his saddlebags, coming out with a small pouch. "For you."

The girl opened the pouch and pulled out a cherry as her sire beamed. "I thank you, my lord."

The husband and wife thanked him until he stopped

them, or he would never make it home this day. The boy had regained some of his color, and stared longingly at Edward's sword.

"You are a good lad to try and fix the wheel, but mayhap you should learn to swim, aye?"

"Yes, my lord." The boy grinned and scampered off, apparently unharmed after almost drowning.

Brom's mouth twitched as they rode away from the mill. "Every marriageable lass in the land will be pounding on your door in the next sen'night."

"Whatever." Edward had come to greatly appreciate the future word.

"The coolers are stocked with bottled water. Does anyone need anything before I head out to pick up lunch?"

Jennifer held a hand up to shade her eyes, and made a mental note to buy a pair of sunglasses in the village. Somewhere during her trip, she'd lost them. Wasn't that always the way? Buy an expensive pair and lose or break them in the first few months. But a cheap pair? Jennifer would have them for years. By now she should have learned her lesson.

In her defense, the expensive ones were so over the top, really black with jeweled flowers across the top. They made her feel like a movie star hiding out in some small town, and so, hoping her credit card would take the hit, she'd splurged. Whoever had found them, Jennifer hoped they loved them as much as she had.

Mark plopped down on one of the coolers with a grunt. "Everyone's set; appreciate you asking. It's nice to have someone around to take care of this stuff. If it was up to me, we'd all be thirsty and hungry."

"I have the same focus when I paint. The world could come crashing down and I wouldn't notice. Thanks again for pointing out the solar showers. Thought I'd end up washing in the stream all summer."

Monica let out a goofy half hiccup, half laugh. "Maybe you should rent a room above the pub so you'll be more comfortable. Sounds like this is a bit much for your delicate sensibilities."

"And miss your charming smile every day? I wouldn't think of it."

The girl scowled and went back to carefully sifting soil from her roped-off section.

Mark's eyes twinkled as he winked at Jennifer before tossing the keys. "You've gotten under her skin."

"Don't I wish it were that easy. Mean girls always come back swinging. I'd better be on the lookout for serious payback after embarrassing her."

He burst out laughing. "Once she put a laxative in my

hot chocolate because I said her laugh sounded like a sick donkey, so you're probably smart to be on guard."

Almost to the beat-up vehicle, Jennifer sniffed. It smelled like Mary was working on something with basil, so she took a slight detour through the grounds, stopping at an open-air tent.

"Do I smell basil?"

Mary dusted her hands off on a white apron. "You have a great sense of smell. Aren't you full from breakfast?"

"Don't get me wrong, breakfast was delicious. Never would have thought of eating beans with breakfast, but I can always eat." At that moment, her stomach let out a growl.

"I'd be as big as a bus if I ate like you."

"My mom's the same way. We fidget a lot."

"I'll have to try it. Certainly works for you." Mary handed her a roll. "This should tide you over. By the time you get back with lunch, this batch of bread will be done. I'll be sure to save you a slice."

The warm air from the ovens hit her teeth as Jennifer grinned. "Wonderful. Need anything from the village?"

"Nope, but thanks for asking."

As she made her way to the parking area, Jennifer spoke to a few of the re-enactors. When she bent down to retie her hiking boots, a shadow fell across the ground in front of her.

"Take care of Morris. I found her neglected in a

farmer's barn."

Charlie was wearing a bright blue t-shirt proclaiming *Shakespeare Lovers Remember You in Their Will.*

"Great shirt."

He looked her up and down. "Great shorts." Then he grinned. "I've been collecting them for a few years. My now ex gave me the first one, and while she's long gone, I like the shirts."

The odd-looking vehicle sat apart on the grass. It was from the seventies, a Morris Minor, and looked like a car and a van had given birth to this odd baby. The burgundy interior matched the exterior. The car even had the expected wooden paneling on the outside.

"She's interesting."

"Hey, she might not be sexy like you, but she's got plenty of storage space in the boot."

Jennifer ignored his look at her butt. He was a harmless flirt and had no idea she wouldn't go near a guy like he or Mark with a ten-foot pole. Not after her mother's track record. Were her shorts too short? She looked down and decided the navy shorts were the same length as the rest of the girls' shorts on site. There was a suspicious-looking spot on the white t-shirt—maybe beans from breakfast? Oh well, not like she was trying to impress a guy.

"I'll take good care of Mrs. Morris." She waved to Charlie and motored down the drive, chanting, "Stay left, stay left." And hoping she wouldn't run off into the ditch while he was watching.

Driving on the left made sense in an older feudal society. Most people, including knights, were right-handed, so they stayed to the left to keep their right arm close to any bad guys. Made sense, and explained why everyone in the good old USA drove on the right. What did the left-handed guys do?

She'd ask one of the students. They'd been a wealth of information so far. And she'd quickly found out they'd tell her all kinds of things while she had them sit for portraits. The sketches were done quickly, but the students liked them, many mailing them home.

Other than dodging a few sheep, she and Morris made it to the village unscathed. Once they crossed over the stone bridge, the church steeple came into view, stark against the bright blue sky. It was a perfect day. The jam she'd spread on her toast at breakfast had come from one of the shops, and so did the tea. She'd be sure to pick up a few items to mail home. Her mom would love the jam for her morning bagel, and with luck the package would arrive by the time she and number four returned home from their cruise.

Chapter Seven

If Shane and her mom didn't last, Jennifer was going to stop calling the guys by name and start using numbers. "Hi, number five, welcome to the family. Keep your boxes—I doubt you'll be here more than a year."

After her dad, the next marriage had lasted three months, and the third actually lasted two years. Now she'd married Shane, and Jennifer had her doubts after watching Shane track every attractive woman in a five-mile radius. The sarcastic voice in her head chimed in. *At least she's willing to put herself out there. Fall head over heels in love, even if it is short-lived. You'd rather float aimlessly through life thinking everything will work out tomorrow and believing you're better off alone.*

"Shut up."

Deciding she wasn't going to argue with herself, she parked the car and meandered through the quaint village, enjoying the shops. The garden behind a church beckoned, and a quick glance at the phone told her there was plenty of time before she needed to pick up lunch.

The cobblestone streets and old buildings made her wonder if anyone famous had ever lived or stayed in the village in the past. Maybe a chivalrous knight or prince?

"I wouldn't mind a Benedict Cumberbatch sighting while I'm here this summer." Jennifer came to the Rabbit and Hound. There were flowers growing in front, and a bell tinkled as she entered. As she stood there inhaling, a woman looked at her like she'd lost her mind.

"Can I help you, love?"

"It smells so good in here, I may move in."

The woman's eyes crinkled when she laughed. "You're from across the pond, then. Whereabouts?"

"Maryland. Baltimore." She tightened the ponytail the wind had tried in vain to undo while she was walking through the village. "I'm Jennifer."

"Edith. The woman who owns the bookshop, Laura, has a son who works in Washington. Not too far from you."

"Not at all. I take the train to DC all the time."

They chatted while Edith helped her pick out an assortment of teas and jams to send home. "The re-enactor group is back, I see. They spend a few months here each year. Odd bunch, but nice enough. Have you found anything of interest up at Somerforth?"

"I've only been here a week, so I don't know what they've found yet. One of the guys said he'd show me the finds tomorrow. Would your friend have any old books with pictures of what the castle might have looked like before it fell?"

"I've got something that might interest you. Back in a moment."

While Edith rummaged in the back, Jennifer snapped a few pictures of the interior of the shop. While walking around she'd had the idea to paint a series with scenes from the village, along with the surrounding landscape and, of course, the ruins.

What must it have been like to live in a simpler time? Spending her days painting and embroidering would have been heavenly, though she'd miss the enormous amount of books and movies available at the touch of a fingertip. And modern conveniences. The voice spoke up. *Right. And what about women's rights, hacking off someone's head with a sword, the plague, no modern medical care, or chocolate or milkshakes?*

"Do you have to ruin my fantasy?"

The voice ignored her. Still, it would be a nice escape for a few weeks. Would someone in the future invent a device to travel back in time? Take tourists to interesting dates and places, allowing them to observe but not interact? That would be the trip of a lifetime.

Jennifer hoped it would come to pass while she was still alive to try it out. Go science.

"Here we are."

Lost in daydreams of wandering through Somerforth with a handsome knight at her side after a busy day slaying dragons, the sound of Edith's voice made her jump a foot. The honorable knight had just about been to swear his undying love for all eternity. It was so real, she had to blink several times to re-enter reality.

Jennifer let out a long sigh. She'd rather stay single and alone forever than end up like her mom. Desperately chasing men and marrying them, only to realize they weren't going to change, or they wanted someone else. The advent of so much technology and connectedness had habituated people to constantly look for the next good thing, never satisfied with who or what they had. Jennifer would rather be alone than risk the heartbreak she'd watched her mother suffer through.

"Jennifer?"

"Sorry. I was somewhere else."

"Somerforth has that effect on many." Edith blew the dust off an old, battered book, the spine coming apart, the dark green cover cracked and faded to a greenish gray, the gold lettering almost completely worn off. When she turned the pages, the intoxicating smell of old books filled the air, mingling with the scent of tea and flowers.

"If I could bottle the way it smells in here, I'd make a

fortune."

"There's nothing like the smell of an old book, is there?"

As Jennifer nodded, Edith added, "My daughter bought me one of those tablets for Christmas. I like the immense number of books I can take with me on holiday, but there's something magical about turning a page and feeling the words seep into your skin as you read."

"Absolutely. I remember when I used to pack one suitcase full of books for a trip. I brought a solar charger so I wouldn't have to worry about a power source."

Edith stopped on a page, and Jennifer caught sight of herself in the mirror. Her mouth hung open, and she looked like she was in a trance. There on the page, staring up at her, was Somerforth Castle. *Exactly* as she'd imagined it.

"The castle was something back in the day. It was immense, and many said it was never the same after Lord Somerforth fell in battle. Time passes; young people go off to live in the city. Not to mention it's terribly expensive to maintain a castle. Eventually, if the grand homes aren't opened to tourists or given over to be preserved, they fall to ruin. Like what happened with Somerforth."

"This is such a treat. I looked everywhere but couldn't find any pictures of what it used to look like. Would you mind if I took a picture of the page?"

"Not at all." Edith stood back as Jennifer captured the image on her phone. The woman ran a finger over the drawing.

"As far as I know, this is the only image of Somerforth. It's not really surprising. There are a great many castles in the world, and this one wasn't historically important." She chuckled. "There was a long-running feud with a clan across the border. Last month the doctor was talking about sheep going missing and turning up at a farm in Scotland. Old habits die hard." Edith touched Jennifer's arm. "You're pale. Sit and I'll pour you a cup of tea."

Jennifer sank down into a floral chair. The shopkeeper brought out a silver tray with two teacups. The delicate cups were decorated with roses, and there was a choice of milk or lemon. "A spot of tea will have you going again."

Sipping the brew, Jennifer focused on taking slow, deep breaths until the sensation of being in two places at once passed. Her overactive imagination was getting the better of her. For a moment she swore she was in a lady's solar, stitching a floral border on a man's tunic.

Tonight she'd better switch from reading historical fiction to something else. Maybe a thriller or cozy mystery. Obviously being in such close proximity to a real castle was sending her imagination into overdrive.

"I feel much better. Sorry to cause a fuss. I'm getting hungry, that's all." She couldn't tell Edith she'd sketched the very same castle in all its glory based on a daydream. Edith would think she was as batty as the re-enactors.

"It's getting late, I'd better pick up lunch and get back. Thank you for the tea and showing me the book. I'll be back again."

"Glad you're feeling better. It was lovely to chat, and next time we'll invite Laura. She always has brilliant book recommendations."

Chapter Eight

The walk down the street to the pub cleared her head. Not wanting to be late, Jennifer was in and out of the pub so fast she barely had time to take in the decor. The drive back was a bit easier, and she hoped soon she wouldn't have to think so hard about which side of the road to drive on. Bags of pies and salads dangling from her arms, she found everyone gathered around a grassy area off to the left side of the grid they'd been working that morning.

"Lunch is here. What's going on?"

The professor popped up. "Set those down and come see. It's quite extraordinary."

Jennifer put the bags on the wooden tables and hurried over as Mark made room for her to squeeze in.

"Monica tripped over a rock, and when she went

down, she caught sight of something in the loose dirt. The rain last week must have uncovered it." Mark pointed, but before he could say anything, Guy appeared, flushed and breathing heavily.

"Heard you found a dagger. Can we see?"

The blade was triangular, tapering evenly from the hilt down to the point. It looked like it had been buried a long time.

"I bet it was lost during a battle."

"Maybe we'll find bones deeper down."

Others weighed in as each person squatted down for a closer look. The pommel bore faint markings that might have been words but had been worn away long ago.

"A brilliant find. Why don't we stop for lunch and celebrate?" The professor beamed as he called for beer to accompany the meal.

Even Monica was in a good mood, and complimented Jennifer on her bracelet as they filled in around the tables. The professor cast a worried look to the dig as thunder sounded in the distance. "Better secure the tarps before the storm hits, and we'll move the meal to the big tent."

"I'll take the beer and you get the food." Mark pulled the coolers by their handles and sprinted across the grass. When she finished moving the food, Jennifer pulled the side curtains so if it did start raining they wouldn't get soaked. As she was counting out napkins and silverware, the wind picked up, carrying the sound of bagpipes.

"Why do I get the feeling you're trying to tell me something?"

But there was no answer as the ghostly piper played on, the last notes ending as she wiped the wetness from her cheeks. The melancholy tune suited the ominous sky, dark clouds rolling over the blue, absorbing the light, replacing it with dark gray, silver, and the palest grayish blue. Despite the warmth of the day, Jennifer shivered.

With a thrust, Edward disarmed his opponent as the man's sword abruptly left his hand. Edward deftly caught it and handed it to the man.

"Better. Now begone." He scowled at the womanly lot before him. He had been too easy on his men of late, mayhap he would run through the entire garrison by twos. 'Twas going to be a most enjoyable morn. He turned to the next man, bored. "Draw your blade."

The man went to his knees. "Bloody hell. Enough."

Edward grinned and clapped the man on the back, sending him into the mud. "A fine display, whelp." Then he turned to what was left of his garrison. "Who else?

None?"

One of his men stepped forward. "Not so fast, my lord. I fear he took it easy on you." The man smirked and Edward quickly stepped forward, laughing as the man's smirk was repressed, replaced with fierce concentration. No one smirked at him.

Swordplay kept his mind off what had transpired. He knew helping Connor last winter would have dire consequences. The bloody Scot had saved Robert's life, and that was how Edward found himself transporting Connor from Highworth Castle to Somerforth, where the man could make his way across the border. He'd come to a grudging respect for the warrior, though it didn't mean he wouldn't kill him if they came face to face in battle.

There were always nobles trying to curry favor with the king, and many had been envious of all that had been bestowed upon the Thorntons. Most forgot how hard Edward had fought to regain the Thornton titles and lands after John lost them over a woman so long ago.

One of the nobles' wives, furious Edward rebuffed her amorous advances, had whispered into her husband's ear and to who knew how many other lovers, telling what she had overheard he and Robert discussing one late eve. Edward found himself summoned to court to face his sire. At least they met privately instead of the spectacle of all the court watching as his king scolded and threatened.

In the end, Edward had to provide more men to fight for his king and pay a fine. He was also banished from court until summoned. 'Twas a minor rebuke, though now he would not rise to favor, as the witch had foreseen. John had known the healer for many years. She'd sworn he would rise to great favor, but it seemed not to be. Never again would his brothers be at risk of losing all; he vowed to do what needs be done to keep them safe.

Wiping the sweat from his brow, Edward drew a bucket of water from the well and dumped it over his head. Tossing his hair back, he heard a soft feminine sound. When he turned, the miller's daughter was standing there holding something in her hands, water droplets on her dress.

"My apologies, mistress. I did not see you there."

She didn't meet his eyes, keeping her gaze on his feet. The girl thrust her offering at him. "I made a pie for you from the cherries, my lord."

He accepted it from the girl as he noted her cheeks turning a ghastly shade of rose. "Smells delicious. I shall enjoy it after supper."

The girl's father came forward. "My daughter wanted to come along when I brought the grain, my lord. See what a fine wife she will make one day."

Wisely, Edward refrained from answering the man, instead scowling at his men, marking which ones were trying in vain to smother their guffaws.

"I will hide this fine pie away from the men." He inclined his head to them.

The man, sensing 'twas time to depart, took his daughter by the arm and led her away. The girl never once looked anywhere but down.

"She will make a good wife. Never gainsay her husband. Give him many sons and mend his hose." Brom chuckled as he leaned on his sword.

"Then you take her as a wife."

His captain blanched. "Nay. Then who would see you did not lose your head in battle?"

"Harrumph. I want a girl who will vex me until I am old and gray and can no longer hear her shouting."

Brom snorted. "Give me a biddable female. The ones that vex you are likely to get you killed."

Edward slapped him on the back. "The very vexing is what makes them so bewitching."

"You are rather feeble to take on a vexing lass. Almost two score."

Edward drew back. "Feeble? I will not be two score for three more years. If anyone is an old meddlesome woman, 'tis you."

Vile slurs were hurled back and forth, making Edward grin. Who knew his captain had such a broad knowledge of insults?

"Come. I require sustenance." He re-sheathed his sword and carried his pie into the hall.

Chapter Nine

Spirits were high on Saturday night. The warm summer night made everyone ready to let loose and relax. A cool breeze ruffled her ponytail, and for the first time since arriving, Jennifer finally felt like she belonged. Part of the group.

Professor VanHemert had left yesterday after lunch to meet with a colleague at Oxford, and the rest of the group was looking forward to a night on the town.

"You coming along?"

She grimaced. "No. I want to capture the ruins at twilight. It's my favorite time of day."

Mark looked bewildered. "You'd rather stay here all alone and paint than come with the lot of us down the pub for a pint? I don't believe you'd willingly deprive yourself of my fine company. There must be some secret boyfriend coming to visit."

"No mystery boyfriend."

The last thing she wanted to do was spend the evening talking and laughing. Surrounded by people and forced to talk to them, feeling like she had nothing interesting to say. After being with the group all day, she was desperate for time to herself to regroup and recharge.

"Next time. I really want to work on my watercolor. The light is so beautiful on the stone this time of day. You all go ahead and have fun."

"Suit yourself." He turned away laughing at something one of the guys said.

She waved goodbye as everyone piled into cars, cranked up the radio, and drove away, leaving her blissfully alone. As silence settled over the estate, Jennifer turned in a circle. The re-enactors had left early that morning, off to perform in a festival, and wouldn't be back for a couple of days. Who knew when she would have the whole place to herself again?

Supplies at the ready, she sat on the folding canvas stool in what she'd come to call her spot in front of her castle. Sure, it was silly to call it *her castle*, but deep in her bones, the stones called to her, singing a song of belonging to this place. So whether in another world or another life, she decided to embrace the feeling and let the creativity flow through her. When the muse showed up, you obeyed or risked her going off pouting and not coming back for ages and ages.

The stack of watercolors in her portfolio was growing. The rose garden and bailey complete. A few of the students had been impressed by the work, so she'd decided to have prints made for everyone before the end of the summer. A couple of originals would go to the professor. One to Mary and Guy of the camp, and a few to keep for herself to mark this magical time in her life.

The feeling this time was somehow special was something she wanted to hold on to when she was back home and working in some office job from nine to five. While she knew her work would never hang in a gallery, it gave Jennifer pleasure. Her mom and dad couldn't understand it. No one in the family was creative. When she was four, her mom found her drawing pictures on the wall with crayons. Instead of yelling, her parents bought her a blank sketch book and markers. Every book she owned had doodles inside. It was a compulsion.

The artists like Monet with his haystacks, who painted the same scene over and over, capturing the changes in light and seasons, spoke to her soul, and so she'd decided she would paint the same view of Somerforth every time she had a chance, noting on the back the date and time of day. By the end of summer she hoped to fill an entire watercolor pad full of paintings and hang them down her wall in a row to show time passing at Somerforth. Too bad she couldn't spend a full year here and capture the rest of the seasons. No, her parents would have her head if she stayed, but it would be lovely...

As she worked quickly against the fading light, laying down color, a shimmer in the grass caught her eye. Jennifer put down the brush, stood, and rolled her shoulders to work out the tension. When she painted, she tended to lose track of time, sitting in one position until she was stiff and creaky.

After the warmth of the day, the wind chilled her, making her wish she'd changed from shorts into a pair of leggings and sweatshirt. Shadows danced across the ground and Jennifer looked up, surprised at how fast the deepening twilight had turned ominous. There was a storm rolling in, and quickly from the looks of it. If the wind didn't pick up, the easel would be fine.

With a glance at the sky again, she decided there was time. Thunder rumbled in the distance, making Jennifer run to the spot where she'd spotted the glint in the grass.

It couldn't be. Jennifer squatted down, hand hovering a few inches above the sword.

"Should I?" Playing out before her was a knight on horseback, riding out from the castle, and she shook her head to clear it.

"Talk about letting the mood of a place get under your skin." Spending a summer at a castle was bound to make anyone see and imagine things—well, unless they were like her big brother, the extremely serious dentist. He would never imagine anything other than a set of perfect pearly whites.

"Somebody's going to be in big trouble for leaving you out here." The professor was pretty easygoing, but this kind of mistake? Leaving a priceless artifact lying in the grass meant somebody would be going home. She should mark the spot and leave it until the group returned from the pub. Find out who was playing with antique swords.

But it might be really late—no, it *would* be late. With the professor gone, they'd close down the pub tonight. And they'd be smashed when they did finally stumble back. What if someone wandered by and stole it while she slept? Then it would be her fault—she'd be the one going home to face the disappointment in her dad's eyes and watch her mother take to her bed for a few days.

"I better not get chewed out for moving you out of the rain." She chewed the corner of her lip. There wasn't time to run back for a clean cloth. The top she wore was splattered with paint, as were the paper towels she'd brought along, and she didn't dare get paint on the beautiful sword. It might be metal and would wash off, but she'd hate for the professor to be upset.

Thunder cracked again, the smell of rain filled the air, and the hair on her forearms stood up, making her itch. A fat raindrop hit her nose. If she hesitated any longer, today's watercolor would be ruined.

The moment she grasped the hilt and pulled it from the dirt, the air seemed to shift. It was heavy. There was no one around, but to be sure, Jennifer took a look around before swinging the sword in front of her. The knight this baby belonged to must have been incredibly fit to swing it around left and right.

Lightning arced across the sky and the biggest emerald she'd ever seen seemed to glow. There was some sort of engraving on the blade. Tilting it back and forth, she squinted at the lettering until her eyes crossed. "Thornton." She looked again. "No way."

Was this some kind of joke? Was Monica going to jump out and laugh at her? This was Edward Thornton's home. No way would his sword be sticking up halfway out of the ground waiting for her to find it. One of the others would have found it. And she'd been coming to this exact spot for over a week to paint. No way she would have missed it.

The wind picked up, and she pushed a stray lock behind her ear. The blade looked much newer than the others she'd seen. On those, the lettering was worn partially or completely off, there were cracks in the jewel if there was one, and the blade looked dull. This sword looked... *Well, let's see.*

Today's watercolor was already ruined. Jennifer ignored it and rummaged in the tote bag, coming up with a cheap scarf she'd purchased in the airport. She blocked the rain with her body, dropped it across the sword, watched it slide down the edge of the blade, and gasped when the two halves were blown away on the wind. It had to be new. No way it would still be that sharp after almost seven hundred years.

Lightning lit up the sky again, and she saw red in the grass. There in the dirt where she'd found the sword was a red stone. Another immense stone. A ruby. The smell of electricity filled her nose and vibrated through the stone and up her arm. The skies opened up, the wind whipping her hair in her face. The easel blew over and was gone.

"No." She ran to pick up the watercolors and brushes, the ruby in one hand and the sword in the other. The ground met her face as she tripped over a rock and went down hard, her fingers skittering down the lettering on the sword as she cried out. Both her palms were skinned and she'd cut the side of her hand. Pushing to her feet, adrenaline coursing thorough her body, Jennifer limped toward the wet supplies, stuffing them in the bag, which had been looped over a stone. Over the thunder and rain, she swore she heard the piper playing.

Lightning hit a tree, the crack so loud she wanted to cower on the ground. As she pulled the bag free from the stone, the ground started to shake. Earthquake?

The ground buckled and she was tossed into the air. Rocks, grass, and roots were all around her, the smell of the earth strong in her nose. The storm raged until finally there was nothing, only gray mist and the ghostly sounds of the piper.

Within the mist, she heard a voice. “To the end of time I will play for you…” The voice faded into the mist as Jennifer said, “I am *not* a Thornton. My name is Jennifer Wilson.”

The voice whispered on the wind, “But you will be.”

Lightning flashed within the mist, the sound of metal screaming made her teeth ache, and the wind swirled around her so strongly that her feet left the ground.

“Make it stop.” She screamed, covering her ears with her hands and closing her eyes tight. “Please, I want to go home.”

Chapter Ten

The next day, Edward and the men were returning from a skirmish across the border, driving a score of cattle. A minor clan allied with Clan Armstrong had dared to take three stag from his lands, and in return, Edward whisked away the clan's cattle. No one stole from a Thornton and got away with it.

On the lookout for angry Scots, the men were already wary when a scream sounded through the wood. Urging the horses forward, they came upon a small hut.

"Brom and Alistair, to me. Ballard, lead the men and cattle back to Somerforth." He dismounted and hit the ground running.

With a booted foot, he kicked the door open, unsheathing his sword. Brom followed, leaving Alistair outside to guard their back in case 'twas a trap. It took a moment for his eyes to adjust to the dim light inside the croft. The home was small but tidy, and as he looked around he saw no threat. Where was the woman?

A makeshift screen in the corner moved, and a woman came forth, saw them, and shrieked.

"We bear you no ill will, mistress." Edward re-sheathed his sword and held out both hands. "We heard a scream and thought you were in distress."

Observing her hands, he gripped the hilt of his sword. "You are covered in blood. What mischief is this?"

The woman looked tired and worn as she wiped her hands on a cloth.

"Nay, my lord. There is no mischief about. You misunderstand. I have given birth."

He had not noticed the bundle in the basket. She held up the babe for them to see.

Brom shrank back in horror from the child, making Edward bite his tongue. "Where is the midwife?"

"There was not time, and I have no money for a midwife."

"Where is your husband?" Edward looked around, expecting to see a Scot running toward him, dirk in his hand and teeth bared.

She narrowed her eyes. "He died fighting you and your men, Lord Somerforth."

"And yet you do not come at me with the knife I see in the babe's blanket."

Her shoulders slumped. “I am no longer angry. There’s been fighting since I was a child. All English are the same, and the Johnston can be a hard man.”

Alistair ducked to enter the hut, and suddenly the room was too small. “There are no animals. Not even a chicken.” He crossed himself as he caught sight of the girl.

Edward spoke in Norman French to Brom. “Send Alistair to catch up with the man. Bring back two chickens, the cow, and the calf for the woman.”

Brom nodded as Edward and Alistair went outside. The woman watched him, holding her babe close. Reaching into the pouch at his waist, he came out with a handful of coins.

“’Tis a sacred act to bring a babe into the world.”

The woman scowled at the coin then him. “I will not lie with you.”

He rocked back on his heels. “I would not ill-use a woman.”

“Then why? I am of Clan Johnston, your enemy.”

“My fight is not with you, a mere woman.”

She snatched the coins from his hand, stowing them away somewhere within the folds of her dress. The woman stared at him for a while then held out the babe.

“Would you like to hold him?”

“Are you not afraid of an Englishman holding your child? I know what the Scots tell their children about me.”

She chuckled, showing a couple of missing teeth. "Aye. The fearsome Lord Somerforth eats small children."

His lips twitched, but he made no sudden moves. "Not enough meat on the bones of such little ones."

The woman slid the small knife into her skirts. "Some English are evil. Some good. Then again, some of my own people are evil. 'Twas a Scot who stole my animals and my food. I care not where you live, only that you have a clean soul." And with that, she thrust the child at him.

As Edward held the babe, he inhaled the sweet scent. "A fine, strong boy. Those we create live and have their own children so that we are never forgotten and may live forever."

There was dust in his eye. He wiped it away before handing the child back to the woman.

"We will take our leave, mistress."

"I am thankful for the coin."

Edward stopped in the doorway. "One of my men is bringing a few chickens, a cow, and a calf for you and the child."

Her eyes were leaking when she followed him outside. Riding away, Brom snorted.

"You look like a lad besotted with his first girl. Marry a girl like that one. She will bear you sons. Make her the lady of Somerforth."

Edward frowned. "The people would not accept a

Scot as their lady." They rode for a while in silence then he asked, "Why do babies smell so sweet?"

His captain coughed. "See how nice they smell when they vomit all over your tunic or shit on you. Then the horrible things smell worse than the cesspit on a hot summer day."

"Mayhap. Still, they do smell rather lovely when they're clean."

No one challenged them on the ride to Somerforth. Likely the Johnston was biding his time. One of the garrison knights stopped them as they entered the bailey.

"Make haste. When bringing up a cask of wine from the cellar, one of the men heard a terrible rumbling. When it stopped, a section of the wall had fallen and there were two doors, one was cracked. Did you know there were secret chambers below?"

"Nay. What's inside?" Edward's father had told he and his brothers tales of hidden passageways when they were growing up, but he did not know Somerforth boasted such things.

"One of the chambers is filled with treasures." The knight rubbed his hands together. The other will not open and..." He crossed himself. "Fearsome sounds are coming from inside the chamber."

"'Tis likely rats." One of the stable lads took the horses as Edward and Brom followed the man to the cellars.

Brom clapped him on the back. “Perchance ’tis a faerie.”

Edward scowled and stomped down the steps.

The steady beating made Jennifer wonder if someone was playing the drums. Nope, just her heart loud in the silence. It was too dark to see anything, yet she couldn’t shake the sensation of being watched.

Reaching out, she felt nothing but air. Everything came back: the storm, the ground opening up, and then darkness. A section of the castle must be here, hidden away until now. Cold seeped into her shorts. Stone. The floor was stone, not dirt. Definitely some kind of room.

Getting to her feet, she tripped over a loose chunk of stone and went down on one knee. The stone was wet from the rain.

“Hello? Anyone?” Jennifer waited for a response but received none. With no phone, she had to guess at the time. Looking up, she saw blackness, so night? Surely Mark and the others would be back from the pub soon and get her out of here.

She felt the stone, and her hands found the wall. Wait until the professor and everyone saw what she found. They would be so excited. “The sword.”

Crawling on hands and knees, Jennifer felt for the blade but found no trace, though she did find a door. Hands on the worn wood, she stood, feeling for a latch to open it and find out where it led.

The latch made a noise but the door wouldn't budge. She couldn't tell if it was locked or stuck from being closed for so long. A noise in the darkness made her shiver.

"Who's there?"

No answer. Hoping it wasn't a rat, she reached up as high as she could, searching for any way to climb out, but there was nothing. Not a single thing to hold on to or stand on. If she were a rock climber maybe she could have done it. Instead she slid down the wall and crossed her legs. When the others came back she'd scream at the top of her lungs, letting them know she was down here.

"My poor easel." The storm had been the worst she'd ever seen. By now the easel and paints were probably at the bottom of the North Sea.

Worst-case scenario? It would be morning before anyone found her. And with that thought, her stomach rumbled.

"Quiet. You're not getting anything until morning, so hush." Oh well, it wasn't like it would hurt her to miss a meal. Her stomach grumbled, disagreeing.

Leaning against the cold stone wall, Jennifer rubbed her arms and legs. She could smell grass and dirt, and imagined what a sight she must be. As she sat pondering a way out of the hidden chamber, she heard another noise.

The sounds were coming from the door, and for a moment she thought she saw light. But that wasn't possible. She was underground, and there was no light coming in the chamber other than moonlight from the gaping hole above her head. Could there be another chamber on the other side of the door? And if there was, what or who was in there?

Those thoughts led her down a path that had fear trying to claw its way out of her throat. She opened her mouth to scream, but no sound came out. And then she heard the unmistakable sound of a key turning a lock.

Chapter Eleven

Edward thought he heard something coming from beyond the door.

"Shall I break it down, my lord?" Alistair placed a hand on the wood.

He bent down, touching the lock. "Aye, break it down." Then Edward paused. Above the lock was the head of a dragon. Where had he seen such a thing before?

While Edward pondered, Alistair returned wielding an axe.

"Hold. I have seen such a mark before." He put a hand on Alistair's arm. "Wait."

Since arriving there had been no more sounds from behind the door. Edward was loath to break it down. He might have need of such a chamber. Somerforth did not boast a dungeon, and in times such as these, perchance it could be useful. He took the steps two at a time up to the hall, startling those going about their day-to-day tasks. Deep in his heart he felt the need not to tarry, to open the door and see what the fates had sent him.

In his chamber, he opened the chest and rifled through the contents. At the bottom, in the corner under his tunics, was what he was looking for. An old ring of keys. One fashioned with the head of a dragon. Running down the stairs, Edward heard a woman's voice.

"Mark? I'm in here."

Alistair and Brom crossed themselves. "'Tis a faerie."

Edward pushed them aside and bent down to fit the key in the lock.

"Nay, Edward. Do not open the door."

"Please help me. I'm trapped in here."

He placed a hand above the lock. "Do not be afraid. I will aid you, lady."

For a moment, he heard nothing. Then the woman spoke.

"Is that French? Guy, is that you? You know I don't speak Norman French. Parlez-vous English?"

Her accent was heinous. Unease crept up his neck, making him reach for his sword. The sound of blades being unsheathed filled the air.

Edward switched to English. "Demoiselle, I am opening the door. Stand back."

"Mark, that is you, isn't it? This isn't funny. Get me

out of here right now."

The key turned halfway and stuck. No matter how he tried, it would not open.

"Bloody hell." He turned to Alistair. "Break it down."

Placing his lips close to the keyhole, Edward said, "Stand away from the door, demoiselle. We must break it down."

The knight swung, hitting the wood with a thud. After several attempts, Edward frowned. "Fetch Thomas."

Alistair wiped his brow. "Damned door is thicker than the walls." He leaned over, hands on his knees, panting. "Do not open the door, I beseech you."

"Womanly fears. 'Tis a girl who found one of the hidden passageways and became lost."

Brom raised a brow.

"My father spoke of such passageways, but I never found the entrance. My brothers and I spent much time searching."

Thomas lumbered down the steps. "I am here, my lord."

The knight was a bear of a man, with the strength to match. Edward had seen him fell five knights in battle without breaking a sweat. Yet the man was as kind and gentle as he was strong. Touched by the faeries, some said.

Edward had taken him in years ago after a battle when his lord was killed. The man had bawled like a babe, but came willingly. He was honest and loyal to a fault.

Six strikes and there was a large hole in the splintered wood.

"Well done, Thomas."

The man grinned and stepped back, leaning against the wall, waiting to see what would come forth from the hidden chamber.

Edward cleared the jagged pieces of wood and stepped back in shock. A woman peered out. Her skin the color of moonlight, her hair like the darkest night, and her eyes the color of an autumn sky. Before he knew what he had done, he made the sign of the cross and dropped his hand to his side. She was beautiful.

"Aid her, dolt." Brom's voice brought Edward back to himself, and he scowled at his captain, his look promising time in the lists later.

Dainty fingers met his outstretched hand, and he jumped back.

"Demoiselle, your skin."

She giggled. "I was painting. It will wash off."

He shook himself and reached out. "Take my hand."

Her hand was small within his, the skin soft as a kitten. Blue eyes looked into his, and she pulled away.

"I don't know you. Who are you?"

"Do not fear me. None will harm you."

"Where's Mark?"

"There is no Mark here." He frowned. Was this Mark

her husband? The thought displeased him. "How did you come to be locked in the hidden chamber, demoiselle?"

"I was painting the ruins. There was a storm and the ground gave way. I fell through and ended up here." She wrinkled her nose, and Edward had the urge to reach out and smooth the lines, but snatched his hand back.

Instead, before she could protest, he took a step forward, leaned in, and lifted her through the broken door.

The men gasped. Edward looked down. "Bloody hell, woman. Where are your clothes?"

Her cheeks turned a fetching shade of pink. "I'm dressed. You're the ones who like to run around playing dress-up."

He called out over his shoulder, "Fetch me a cloak to cover the lady."

"It is kind of chilly down here, thanks. I don't recognize you. Guy said a few new guys would be joining his group, but I thought it would be after they came back from the festival." She looked over his form, and he wondered if she found him pleasing.

"You guys really look the part, huh?"

Confused by her words, Edward looked her over, shocked at the amount of her he could see.

"Is this Mark or Guy your husband? Where is he?" He heard a sound, and turned to see Alistair holding out a cloak while the others gaped at her. Narrowing his eyes, he snatched the cloak and wrapped it around her.

"Why are you not dressed..."

She put her hands on her shapely hips and sneered at him. "Let me guess, you're one of those chauvinist pigs who thinks all women should wear long skirts and sleeves and be pregnant and barefoot?" She stepped forward, poking him in the chest. "Well?"

He knew the phrase *chauvinist pig*. 'Twas a favorite slur of James' wife Melinda when he displeased her.

Could she be? Nay, 'twas a jest.

"Are you a wench from Winterforth sent to vex me? Where is Christian?"

Her eyes narrowed, the pale blue turning darker. "Did you just call me a hooker?" She rolled her eyes. "This whole staying in character thing is a bit ridiculous, don't you think?" Without waiting for him to answer, she frowned up at him. "Now help me out of here so I can find my easel and paints." Then she muttered, "Hopefully the storm hasn't blown them clear to Scotland by now."

Scotland? Swords pointed at the woman. Edward slapped Alistair's blade away.

He lifted the blade again. "She is a spy. Scottish wench."

"Lock her up." Brom had re-sheathed his blade, but kept his hand on the hilt. "Repair the door and lock her away."

The woman favored his captain with such a

disdainful gaze, Edward almost laughed.

"Seriously. A spy? And I'm not Scottish, hello, no accent. I'm American. Enough with the games. This is 2016 not 1300." She peered at them, looking as regal as a warrior princess. Then she reached out and touched his tunic. "This is Somerforth Castle, right?"

"Aye. From whence do you hail?"

"America. Land of the free..." She blew out a breath. "And lately, home of the crazy."

America. She was one of them. A future girl. Edward thought he might faint, but knights, especially fearsome knights such as he, did not swoon. Ever.

Chapter Twelve

Edward turned to the men. "Alistair. You and Thomas will say nothing of our guest. I will speak with you anon."

Thomas willingly went up the steps. Alistair paused, looking back at him. "No good will come of her being here. Send her back to whence she came."

"Harrumph." Edward nodded to Brom, who moved to stand at the bottom of the stairs in case any came to find them. Then he turned back to the woman. "Where in America do you come from?"

"Maryland. Baltimore." She waved a hand. "Let me see if I've got this? You think you're in medieval England? And we're close to the border of Scotland, which is why I must be a spy?" The woman rolled her eyes. "That sound about right?"

Edward felt the corner of his mouth twitch. He had heard such a tone before from all of his brothers' lady wives. 'Twas what he called mockery and they called sarcasm.

She wrapped his cloak more tightly around her pleasant form. "Quit fooling around. I'm dirty and hungry and I want a shower before Monica comes back tonight and hogs the last of the hot water. It is still night, isn't it?"

"Is this Monica an Armstrong?"

"What? No. She's a mean girl." She let out a snort and threw up her hands. "Whatever. I get cranky when I'm hungry."

Whatever. Yes, she was a future girl.

"'Tis almost time for supper. And aye, this is England and we are the only stronghold between that savage country."

"Don't really care about the stronghold crap. Take me to your leader so I can get back to my day, okay? No wonder I'm hungry. I've been down here all night." The woman scowled at him. "Hurry up. I have things to do. Just wait until I see Mark and the rest of them. Leaving me down here all night. They can fetch their own damn water for the rest of the week. Jerks."

Edward made the fetching shrew a small bow. "I am the leader. Edward, Lord Somerforth, at your service, demoiselle."

She blinked at him, unsure and muttered, "Great.

Next he'll tell me his name is Thornton and I'm in his castle. Sooo not funny."

Edward knew the witless look on his captain's face must be the same on his own visage. Brom unsheathed his sword as the woman took a step back, and Edward noticed her strange footgear.

"Aye, I am Edward Thornton." Christian knew he wanted a future girl. Disappointment pierced his breast as he met Brom's gaze. "Likely Christian sent her. One of his fugitive brides. 'Twas a fine jest. I will repay the whoreson next I see him."

"Who is Christian? A bride?" She shuddered. "I'm not married. No way."

"Christian Thornton, Lord Winterforth? My youngest brother." Edward watched her face as he spoke.

"Never heard of him, but I have heard the name Thornton." The woman pulled some kind of thread from her arm and pulled her long hair into one of the fetching ponytails he'd seen Anna wearing the last time he saw her. She pointed to his sword. "If you're Lord Somerforth, how do you have your sword? I found it half buried out in the field before I ended up here." She tapped her full lips then pointed at his blade. "Does that one have your name engraved on it?"

Edward unsheathed his sword. "This is the sword you found in a field?" He scoffed. "I would never leave my sword in the mud."

She peered closely at the blade and nodded. "Exactly

that sword." She reached out to touch the wording, but he grasped her hand before she could touch the blade.

"Careful, 'tis sharp."

She looked at him with mistrust. "Do you have a piper?"

He paled. "I did."

"Where is he? He's been playing for me."

"He died saving Charlotte. My brother's wife."

She reached out, but instead of touching him, she pulled her hand back. "I'm sorry."

"He played for you? You saw him?"

There was sorrow in her face when she said, "I never saw him, but I heard him several times. Everyone at the camp said he only played for the Thornton women, but I told them how silly that was. I'm not a Thornton. My name is Jennifer. Jennifer Wilson."

Brom arched a brow. It had to be.

"What is this camp?"

"Sheesh. You guys really like to stay in character, huh? I was staying at the ruins for the summer, working for the professor. I'd been painting."

"Ruins?"

"Funny. The ruins of Somerforth."

He swayed. "My home no longer stands?"

"It fell hundreds of years ago." She frowned at him. "There aren't any Thorntons left, as far as I know."

His voice sounded rough to his ears. "What year did you say it was, Mistress Jennifer?"

"Fine. I'll play along. It is 2016, my annoying lord."

Brom's shoulders shook as he covered his mouth. Catching sight of Edward, he coughed. Edward tried to scowl but failed.

"What's so funny?"

Brom wiped his eyes. "Apologies, lady. Tell her, Edward."

"Tell me what?"

Edward said quietly, "'Tis the Year of Our Lord 1334."

She laughed then stopped, her eyes huge. "You're not acting? Swear it?"

"I vow it." He held out his arm. "Come to the hall, where 'tis more comfortable. You are shivering."

The woman named Jennifer blinked at him.

"Are you coming, mistress?"

She straightened. "Of course I am. Who wouldn't after that statement?"

Her hand looked small on his arm, and he felt the chill through his tunic.

"Could you take me outside? I need to see."

"Aye, mistress."

He led her through the hall, Brom stopping to speak to several of the men. Her grip tightened on his arm as she took in his hall, the people. A small sound came from deep within her. She swayed, and he did not think; he swept her up into his arms.

"I... This is a real castle."

Outside, she gasped, trembling in his arms.

"Formidable, isn't it?"

She wiggled. "Please put me down so I know I'm not hallucinating. I need to feel the ground with my own two feet."

He frowned but did as she bade him, staying close in case she swooned. The woman turned in a circle, stepping away from him and into the path of two of his guardsmen practicing swordplay. The whoosh of a blade stole the breath from him.

"Damnation," he thundered. "You almost took her head."

One of the men shrugged. "She should have ducked."

The blow Edward dealt the man sent him stumbling back, rubbing his jaw. The future girl slowly turned in circle after circle, mouth agape.

"'Tis a difficult thing, the knowledge things are not as we expect them to be."

She gripped his arm, her mouth opening and closing. Then her eyes rolled back and he caught her, sweeping her into his arms as she swooned. A gasp had him scowling at the men who were gaping at her bare legs. He tucked the cloak firmly around her and strode through the courtyard as people stopped to gape, but none said a word, fearful of his foul temper.

Brom ordered the men about and followed Edward, snorting and mumbling.

"You take sport in my discomfort."

Cheerily, Brom replied, “Aye. I do.”

Edward stomped up the stairs, entering the empty chamber next to his.

“Bring me wine,” he bellowed as he laid her on the bed.

His captain failed to suppress a guffaw.

“Do not say a word, dolt.”

The wretched whoreson turned away, shoulders shaking before he gave up and laughed until his eyes leaked.

“Seems the fates have a sense of humor. They sent the future girl you wanted.” He pretended to think. “What was it you said? ‘The vexing makes them bewitching’ or some such drivel?”

Edward sighed. “She is glorious.”

His captain pursed his lips. “Will you send word to your brothers? She should meet the others.”

The woman was asleep on the bed. The need to protect her rose within him. Her hair spread across the pillow, the strands like the finest silk. She was fiery and would make him a perfect wife. She mumbled in her sleep, throwing an arm across her face. The cloak gaped open and he looked his fill. A fine, shapely form, long legs, and a fine, plump...

“Edward?”

“Aye?”

“You’re drooling on her.”

“I do not drool.” He frowned and stomped from the

room, passing a girl carrying a pitcher of wine. “Leave it for her.”

The girl almost dropped the wine in her haste to flee his foul humor. His brothers’ wives led them about by the nose. Edward would not allow such behavior. She would be his lady and obey him as her lord. For he was the most feared knight in the land and knew what was best for her.

Chapter Thirteen

Jennifer's eyes fluttered open. She was in a bed in a very authentic-looking medieval chamber.

"I don't understand." The smell of horses and grass filled her nose. It was coming from the cloak she was wrapped in. It smelled like *him*. And just like that, everything came crashing back.

"Medieval England." Somehow she'd fallen through the earth and wound up at Somerforth in the year 1334 and met the lord of the castle, Edward Thornton. If he hadn't taken her outside to show her his home, with people going about their day-to-day lives, horses, men fighting with swords, and the castle...she would have thought she'd hit her head and was dreaming. The castle looked like she'd imagined and sketched.

"Oh no." All her watercolors and sketches were

probably ruined by the storm. It was daytime, so did that mean the students had figured out she was missing? Did time work the same way? Maybe she'd only been gone for a minute? Or worse, days or weeks? It would take a while for her parents to figure out why she hadn't responded to their messages. They were so busy that they really wouldn't worry until she didn't come home at the end of the summer.

"Stop being negative. You got here; you can get back." Then another thought occurred. If she went back now she'd miss out on the opportunity of a lifetime to experience life in medieval times.

The door opened, and a man stuck his head in, blanched, and slammed the door.

"Wait." But he was already gone. The floor was uneven. No, she was dizzy. Gripping the post at the corner of the massive bed, Jennifer took a few deep breaths. Who knew how long she'd stood there thinking about the unbelievable fact she'd somehow traveled through time when the door banged open again and the man who smelled like a fantasy strode in like he owned the place. Which, come to think of it, he did.

"Are you going to swoon again?"

Like it was her fault? Anyone would have fainted finding out they'd woken up almost seven hundred years in the past. She removed her death grip from the bed and glared at the hottie.

"No. I'm fine."

He nodded and picked up a pitcher she hadn't noticed. The bossy man practically pushed her down into a chair and handed her a beautiful goblet. Before she could examine it, he poured a dark-colored liquid into the cup. The tangy smell of wine filled her nose.

"Drink."

She took a sip, then a few more, letting the alcohol work to calm her frazzled nerves. While he watched her, she looked around the room. It was sparsely furnished with a stool, a chair, a small chest at the foot of the bed, and, of course, the huge bed. The thing could sleep four comfortably. It had rich-looking curtains tied to the post at each corner. The man must have decided she wasn't going to fall over. Seeing such a massive man sitting on the small stool made her smile.

He took her hand in his, rough calluses scratchy against her skin. The huge hand dwarfed hers.

"You know where you are?"

"Somerforth Castle."

He beamed at her as if she had just spelled *cat* for the first time.

"And *when* you are?"

Before speaking, she drained the wine and pointed to the pitcher. He absently refilled it.

"If I remember correctly, you said I'm in 1334?" There, she'd gotten the date out without her voice breaking. Saying it out loud made it more real. Final. As if seeing the tableau wasn't enough, she had to own the date by speaking it out loud.

The intensity of his gaze made her sit up straight.

"What?"

"I am waiting to see if you faint again."

"I bet you would have passed out too if you came to 2016. Cars, trains, TV."

He scowled, which he seemed to do a lot in the short time since she'd met him. "I do not faint. 'Tis womanly."

The other man stood, feet shoulder width apart, arms crossed as if he were expecting an attack at any moment. He made her nervous.

Edward leaned forward. "Tell me everything that happened. All you can remember."

"I told you I was painting. The storm came in fast, and I saw something in the dirt when the lightning flashed." She pointed. "It was your sword. Then the sky opened up, the ground trembled, and when I woke, I found myself in the chamber where you rescued me."

The man nodded, and she wondered why he wasn't throwing her in the dungeon or calling for wood and fire, but before she could ask, he steepled his fingers under his chin.

"Where did you get those?" He pointed to the cuts on her hands.

"Oh, I'd almost forgotten." She held up her hands, looking at the cut on the side of one hand and the scrapes on the other that were already scabbing over. "I had your sword in my hand when I fell and cut myself.

My other hand scraped on the stones." She fought with herself to really believe she was sitting in a chair inside a medieval chamber, having a conversation with a guy who looked like a scary, much rougher version of Chris Hemsworth playing Thor. He certainly had the movie-star looks, and those cheekbones could slice paper. Jennifer looked at him out of the corner of her eye, noting the chiseled jaw and the forest-green eyes. What was he? Maybe six four? And massive. From the wide shoulders that tapered to a trim waist to thick legs encased in hose. Every time he moved, the muscles flexing. Bet he could rip a tree down with his bare hands. They sure didn't make 'em like that in her day.

"I have to ask. Why aren't you calling for a priest to burn me at the stake or something?" Jennifer held up her hands. "Not that I'm complaining. It just isn't at all the reaction I expected."

He pressed his lips together. The man behind him came forward.

"Tell the lass."

"Tell me what?"

"You're not the first future girl to appear on Thornton lands."

Chapter Fourteen

"Wait. What did you mean I'm not the first?" Jennifer jumped up from the chair so fast that he had to catch her before she fell on her face. Strong arms held her close, his scent sending shivers through her. A man like Edward could make her feel cherished, safe. And then the doubt started.

"You had me going until the whole *there are others* bullshit." She pulled away from him, scowling at both men. "Did Monica drug me after I fell in the hole? It would explain how you had time to stage this whole thing. I bet that witch took me to another castle and had all the re-enactors play their part." She poked Edward, or whatever his name was, in the chest. "Admit it. You're an actor." Jennifer shook her head. "You're good, I'll give you that much."

While he and the scary guy, who obviously was supposed to be the underling in this farce, argued, she bolted for the door, flung it open, and ran down the corridor, boots clomping on the stone and the cloak fluttering behind her.

At the bottom of the stairs, she ran outside as people startled and scattered out of her way. Outside, she skidded to a stop.

She muttered, "Be logical. Time travel isn't real, no matter how convincing he made it sound." Somerforth was a ruin, so they'd taken her somewhere else, but where? Too bad she hadn't looked up where other castles were located, other than the famous ones. *Look around, dummy—could mean girl Monica really have pulled something like this off? And all because she's jealous Mark liked you better?*

A snort escaped. "I don't even like him like that. Okay, let's take a closer look."

Jennifer walked up to the closest person and fingered their clothing as the woman shrank back, crossing herself. The cloth felt rough enough to be authentic. The seams would tell. No way they'd have all the fake medieval clothes handmade; it would be too expensive. She peered closely at the seam, and it was immediately apparent the stitches were done by hand.

The woman pulled away.

"Sorry."

The wind shifted and Jennifer wrinkled her nose.

Face it, cupcake: somehow you've ended up in the past.

All the way across the bailey, through the portcullis and across the drawbridge, no one stopped her. There. The spot where she'd painted the ruins. Even as she knew what she'd see when she turned, her mouth went dry. It wasn't fake. She had been right to believe Edward. There before her stood Somerforth Castle exactly as she'd sketched it, and as he'd shown her before Jennifer had passed out. Her fingers twitched, aching to put the rustic scene to paper.

Lost in thought and finally truly accepting she had done the impossible, tremors racked her body as she noticed it had grown dark. Nope, it was a massive shadow. The shadow in question cleared its throat.

"Demoiselle?"

"Jennifer," she absently corrected.

"Jennifer. You are scaring my people. Perchance you could come inside the hall and rest a bit after your...long journey?"

Solemn green eyes looked at her, and she wanted to burst into tears and throw herself in his arms. But she refrained.

"You're probably right. That's a good idea."

Lost. Adrift. Orphan. Words passed through her head as they walked. She was almost seven hundred years away from her family and everything she knew. When the professor found the chamber, would he or one of the students come through the same portal she had? But then, why didn't she go back right away? Did it only work at certain times?

Jennifer was so wrapped up in coming to terms with her situation that she tripped again, and would have gone sprawling if he hadn't swung her up in his arms. Again.

"Oh. You don't need to carry me. I can walk."

He arched a brow. "You are overtired and I will not have you fall and weep, making my ears bleed."

And that was that. He jogged through the hall, ignoring the curious stares. This time he went a different way, and came to a door where he stopped. She peeked out from his shoulder to see one of his men. Alistair or something?

"No one is to enter."

"Aye, my lord."

The room was masculine and carried the smell she'd already come to associate with him. It was his study—or solar, it was called. Just think if the professor could see Somerforth in all its glory.

Edward bellowed for wine, causing her to flinch at the sound. He sat down in a chair and kept her on his lap, holding her close as she finished warring with herself over her new reality. A delayed reaction after she thought she'd accepted it? Who knew?

The door opened and a goblet was thrust into her hand.

She blinked. "Is this silver?"

"Aye."

The wine was chilled and slid down, soothing her scratchy throat. Then her stomach, annoyed there was only liquid, let out a growl.

He peered at her and bellowed over his shoulder, "I am hungry." The silence stretched out, not uncomfortable, but like he somehow knew she needed him not to talk while she came to grips with what she had experienced.

A boy brought a trencher with bread, cheese, and fruit, making her mouth water.

"Eat."

"Will you let me down now?"

He stood and deposited her in the chair. While she ate, he paced back and forth across the room, glancing at her. Not in a creepy stalker way, more with concern. The goblet never went below half before he refilled it.

She wiped her mouth with the large linen napkin, squared her shoulders, and made a decision. To stay. For a week. Two at the most.

During that time, she'd soak up every detail of medieval life she could. Then she'd go down to the chamber, go through whatever portal was located there, and tell everyone about her grand adventure.

The sarcastic voice spoke up. *Great. How exactly are you going to get back to the future? Not like there's a time machine in the chamber. How do you know there is a portal? Maybe it was some kind of freak accident.*

"I'm sorry I kind of lost it earlier. Guess the whole time-travel thing wasn't as easy to accept as I thought." Jennifer jumped up. "Wait. You said there are others like me. How did they travel through time? How do I go back? Could I bring others? The professor would die to see your home."

Edward held up his hands. "I do not have time for womanly drivel, so I will tell you what I know."

But the damn door opened and the scary guy came in. What was his name? Right. Brom. A small snicker escaped. Like the guy on *Game of Thrones.* She tilted her head. He kind of looked like him, except this Brom was definitely more lethal and scarier.

Chapter Fifteen

"We have a guest."

What was the bastard doing in his hall?

Brom grimaced. "No one saw him arrive." He rubbed his jaw.

The Scot grinned. "Aye. I caught yer fine captain unawares in the stables with a tasty kitchen wench."

The insolent whoreson caught sight of Jennifer. "Apologies. I dinna realize you had such a bewitching lass hidden away."

Brom stepped forward and Edward shook his head. A look passed between them, and Edward would wager the Scot would find himself facing Brom in the lists when none were around to gape at the spectacle.

"Who have we here?"

She turned that fetching shade of pink, and Edward

wanted to stomp over to the fire and haul her away.

"Jennifer."

"A lovely name for a lovely lass." He kissed her hand, ignoring Edward. "Connor McTavish."

He turned to Edward. "Where did ye find this one? How do you and your brothers keep finding such wonders?"

"Stay away from her, Connor. She is from far away and under my protection."

"Aye, I can tell." He eyed Jennifer's legs, which had come uncovered again. Damnation, he hadn't had time to find her proper clothing yet. She leaned away from him when he stomped over and reached for the cloak. Did she think he would strike her?

"Cover yourself. 'Tis scandalous the way you are dressed. Men in your time must come to blows every time a fetching wench prances by them."

"I don't have anything else to wear," she said coolly.

And the bloody Scot had the impudence to laugh at him.

"You. What the bloody hell do you want of me now?"

Connor crossed his arms and leaned against the wall. "I wish to know Mistress Jennifer much better."

Edward bellowed for Alistair. "Find her something to wear to supper." His man turned to leave. "Nay. Take her with you, dolt." He looked to Jennifer. "Go. Now." And she made him feel like an arse when he saw the look of hurt on her face.

"Fine. I'll go, but we haven't finished our conversation," she said.

"Alistair?"

"Aye, my lord?"

"Guard her with your life."

The man nodded. "I vow it."

Edward waited until she'd left with Alistair before turning back to Connor. The vexing Scot was looking at him with an expression Edward did not care for.

"You care for her."

Running his hands through his hair, Edward refused to answer. Not until he told Jennifer he wished to woo her.

"Why are you here?"

"The Johnston woman you aided. Her husband saved me from the sword of an English bastard. Seems I now owe you a life. Again." Connor pushed off from the wall. "I did not know her man died or that she was starving. I will see to her welfare." He clapped Edward on the shoulder. "Be wary. The Johnston and the Armstrong want your head. They are plotting against you and Somerforth."

"Let them come." Then he grasped Connor, forearm to forearm. "You have my thanks for the warning."

"Aye. 'Tis too dangerous to trust a messenger with such news. Too many spies about." He lifted a tapestry on the wall, and Edward heard a click.

"Bloody hell."

Connor grinned. “Our sires knew one another. ’Tis how I come and go. You needs learn all of the secrets of your hall.”

Grudgingly, Edward agreed.

“Edward?”

“Aye?”

“Jennifer is a rare woman. ’Tis not safe here for her. Might you send her back?”

He blew out a breath. “Mayhap I should, but not yet.”

Cold air blew in through the passage. Edward watched the Scot leave, and swore under his breath. The fates must be filled with mirth over such doings.

Jennifer woke to the rumble of male voices. It had been an incredibly long day. All she wanted was something to eat and then to sleep for about a week. Lethargy filled her. Was it jet lag? Or the right term might be time-travel lag? Was that food she smelled?

Yawning, she caught sight of Edward. He finished talking to his men and sent them out of the solar. The smile he turned on her, well, she felt it all the way to her toes. Earlier, he'd been jealous of Connor paying attention to her. If it got out how many drop-dead hunky men were in the past, there'd be mayhem. Every single woman in the world would want to travel through time to snag her own man. Jennifer sniffed. Not that she cared.

Sure, keep telling yourself that, cupcake, said the voice in her head. Edward stalked over to her like a hungry lion eyeing a particularly tasty gazelle. She gulped.

"I did not wish to wake you."

Her stomach gurgled and the corner of his mouth pulled up as if tugged by an invisible string. Oh boy. With those sexy, crinkly lines at the corner of his eyes when he smiled... She stopped. And when he grumbled they showed up too. Paired with the drool-worthy accent and deep, gravelly voice that rumbled through her every time he spoke, how was it he wasn't married?

Could he be gay? He had to be mid-twenties to mid-thirties. He was titled, lived in a freaking castle, and was rich. He should have had a wife and a boatload of kids running around. Her heart sank. The guy wasn't jealous Connor was flirting; he was jealous because he wanted Connor. Oh well, at least she wouldn't have to worry about falling for him.

Liar. You already are. Talk about picking the unavailable ones.

"Shut up."

"Pardon, demoiselle?" He frowned at her.

"Never mind." She waved a hand about. "Did you

mention food?"

He picked up a platter as she hopped up to help, carrying the jug of wine and goblets over to the small table.

"Where did Connor go?"

Edward's hand hovered over the meat. "'Tis fine to mention his name to me or to Brom, but not to the others. He's a Scot."

"You must miss him." She thought for a moment, understanding dawning. "Got it. The whole Second War of Scottish Independence."

He gaped at her.

"Fudge. Forget what I said."

"There is always fighting. The only change is the country. Soon 'twill be France."

Jennifer chewed, enjoying the savory vegetables. "The Hundred Years' War." She clapped a hand over her mouth. What was wrong with her? It was like showing off for the teacher you had a crush on.

"Explain."

"The Hundred Years' War goes from 1337 to 1453, if I remember correctly. Really, I shouldn't say anything. What if I tell you and somehow you change history?"

While he thought about what she'd said, Jennifer thought about what else was coming. The Black Plague. No way did she want to be stuck here when the plague burned through.

"Now that we're alone, would you finally explain

what you meant about 'others'? I've been dying to know."

Edward leaned back in the chair, long legs stretched out in front of him and crossed at the ankle.

"Brom and Connor know of what I am about to speak, but no others. Give me your word you will not tell anyone."

She crossed her heart. "Promise."

Nodding, he looked into the flames. "I am the eldest of five brothers. Christian and I are unwed; the rest... they married lasses like you."

"You want to marry?" She resisted the urge to smack her forehead. He told her there are other time travelers and she was stuck on the "is he or isn't he" question?

"Aye. I hope to marry soon." He blinked at her.

"So you're not... I mean..." Finally she gave up on tactful and blurted out, "You're not gay?"

"Aye. I can be. As eldest I must take care of my brothers, see them wed and cared for. I am not a fool, but I make merry."

She brightened. "Oh. No. I thought maybe you liked men." He looked confused, so she tried again, the mortification coursing through her, but it was too late to take it back.

"You know. To kiss. And to...you know...lust with." Her cheeks burned.

Edward jumped up, striding across the room. "You thought I... With Connor?" He narrowed his eyes at her.

"Bloody hell. What kind of men are in your time? No wonder you are unwed and so old."

She was so happy he wasn't gay that it took a moment for the insult to sink in. "Old?" Jennifer screeched. "I'm not old. I'm only twenty-seven. Lots of women in my time wait until their thirties to get married." She set the goblet down with enough force for the wine to slosh over the edge. "Marriage is different. Men marry and then leave. I'd rather be alone." She sneered at him. "What are you, thirty? Forty? Talk about old."

"I have thirty-seven years," he said stiffly.

Seeing the hurt on his face, she calmed a bit. "I'm sorry," she said quietly. "I made an assumption. Can we forget everything I said and talk about your brothers?"

"Harrumph." He paced a few more times before sitting back down, elbows on his knees. "Women of your time have odd ideas."

"We do. But it can be confusing in my time." She waved a hand. "Never mind. You were saying?"

"All of my brothers' wives and James and William's wives are from the future." He whispered the last word.

"Really? How?"

Jennifer vibrated in her chair as Edward explained about each of the women who had traveled through time. So it was possible to go back, though none of them had done so. Each had made the decision to stay. At least, that was what they all thought. No one had actually gone back, so while Edward thought it was possible, none of them were sure.

Because of the fighting, he wasn't sure when she might talk with them. But now she knew that his sword was the key to going back. It would be easy enough to nick her hand for the drops of blood. The next storm, she could go home.

"When we have another storm, can you help me go back?"

He looked like he wanted to say something, but changed his mind. "Aye. When we have a terrible storm, I will aid you."

Chapter Sixteen

Jennifer had never been dressed by someone else. It was a strange feeling, standing naked before another person while they helped you into your clothes.

A tiny part of her almost wished Edward was unavailable. He was gruff and charming, and had gone out of his way to be kind to her when he could have thrown her in his dungeon or had her burned at the stake. Talk about a deadly combination of perfection.

There were others here in the past. Just like her. She and Edward had talked long into the night last night, and on and off all day today as he kept her close. It had been fascinating following him around, watching him interact with his people.

It would be smart to keep her walls high and guard them as closely as Edward's men guarded Somerforth.

No way could she afford to let him in. A man like him would break her heart into a million pieces, she just knew it. To still be single after all these years. She'd seen the way the serving girls had giggled and blushed. Not that she expected him to be a monk or anything, but he was probably a total ladies' man. Not the guy for her. No matter how much she was already attracted to him.

The chemise the girl pulled over her head was beautifully embroidered. Jennifer could sew by machine. There were many times she'd tried to embroider by hand, but she didn't have the patience. The amount of time it took to create such a small design boggled the mind. And here she stood fingering exquisite embroidery all around the hem and neckline of the chemise.

"Did you do the embroidery?"

The girl smiled shyly. "Aye, lady."

"It is lovely. I can't embroider at all."

"Truly?"

She shook her head as the girl pulled a tunic over the chemise, and then a gown went over that. The outfit was finished off with a belt and a small pouch at her waist. Not that she had anything to put in it. Maybe paintbrushes, if she could figure out where to get some.

And parchment. Maybe she could do some paintings in exchange for supplies? Too bad she wasn't holding on to her tote full of paints when she fell.

The girl did Jennifer's hair in pretty braids, fastened

at the nape of her neck with beautiful silver combs.

"Thank you."

"I'm glad you are pleased, lady. Shall I take you to the hall?"

"No, I know the way."

This would be her first meal in the great hall with everyone. As she made her way down the stairs, she felt beautiful. At the landing, she stopped. Did she turn left or right?

"Left it is." Yep. She was talking to herself again. Jennifer's friends said it was because she lived alone. Who knew? It was something she'd done since she was a little girl.

At the bottom of the stairs she found herself in the kitchens. People were crazy busy, so she edged out of there and turned into what she thought was a corridor but must have been a couple of rooms serving as the larder. Hearing voices, she was about to call out when something in the tone of one of the voices stopped her.

It wasn't Norman French. Closing her eyes, she focused on the voices. Gaelic. And not Connor. What on earth were two people doing in the larder speaking Gaelic? Jennifer risked a peek around the corner then pressed back into the wall. The girl looked young, barely a teenager, with red hair and freckles across her nose. The man looked significantly older, with brown hair and a wicked scar running down his neck.

They were coming. Jennifer looked around and just

in time darted behind several barrels. She could see through a tiny crack where the barrels weren't pushed all the way together, and watched as the girl checked to see if the coast was clear. Then she sent the man out, followed, and immediately called out to people in the kitchens, distracting everyone so they wouldn't see the man slinking out.

One of the servants caught sight of Jennifer as she stepped out of the pantry in time to see the redheaded girl scowling at her. The servant frowned. "Lady? Why are you not in the great hall, where Lord Somerforth waits?"

The man with the scar was gone. Jennifer gave the girl a look as if to say, *I know you were up to something.*

"Maude, fetch the bread." The girl made a face and turned away.

"I got lost on my way to the hall."

The servant nodded. "Somerforth is overlarge." The woman led Jennifer to the great hall and up on the dais where Edward was sitting.

"I am pleased the dress fits. The color reminded me of the darker blue in your eyes. You look most fetching."

Jennifer felt the heat travel up her cheeks and, against her will, found herself smiling. He was a force of nature. When he smiled, it lit up the entire room.

"It's gorgeous. Thank you." She didn't tell him how much the other dress itched and kind of smelled. At least Brom had found her a dress, even if it came from a village wench. The one she wore now came from Edward. To know he'd picked it out with her in mind made her heart flutter.

There was a shallow basin of water on the table, and as she watched she noticed people washing their hands, so she did the same. As her mom said, *If you're not sure what fork to use, watch everyone else.*

There were pewter plates on the table. "You don't use the trenchers at supper?"

"We do, but tonight we have an honored guest, so we feast."

"Who?" She stopped at the look on his face. "Me?"

"Aye." He poured the wine in her goblet and served her the choicest morsels, sharing his eating knife. There were tablecloths on the tables and large linen napkins for everyone, though instead of putting them on their laps, most people had them over their shoulders.

The wine was chilled and kept in pottery jugs. His men and the other diners had pottery cups instead of the silver goblets. She already knew a few trenchers would go to the dogs and the rest taken to the poor. Thank goodness she'd been found by the lord of the castle and not a peasant. What a different experience it might have been.

There were cherries in honey, and she wanted to take the whole bowl for herself. Mustard and salt was available, and most of the dishes were delicious. Edward obviously had lots of money, as evidenced by the spices and state of the castle. Money made a big difference in these times—heck, even in her own time the divide between rich and poor was becoming greater and greater.

The hearths in the room were huge. The floors gleamed and there was a mosaic inset in the middle of the floor that looked like it belonged in a museum. It must have dated from roman times. Jennifer remembered the professor talking about the mosaics and the first earl. To see them in person...she itched to sketch them.

"Lady? What are you doing?"

Chapter Seventeen

Jennifer was tracing the design on the tablecloth with a fingertip as Edward watched her.

"I was just thinking how much I'd like to paint your home."

"You are a painter in your time?"

"I don't make a living painting. It's difficult to do so. In fact, I don't have a job. Hopefully I was going to get one when the summer was over." She went on to tell him about the dig and how she'd painted the various scenes.

"Would you paint Somerforth?"

"Are you kidding? I'd love to." She took his hand, heard a noise, and found several pairs of eyes watching her intently. Snatching her hand away, she felt the heat bloom across her chest.

“Then it shall be so. After you break your fast on the morrow, I would show you around the gardens. The roses are in bloom.”

“I’d like that. I saw what was left of the rose garden…” She looked around to see if anyone had overheard.

Edward leaned closer. “The garden still stands?”

“It is overgrown, the walls falling down, but some of the roses are still there. I could smell them before I ever saw them.”

Then his face brightened as a huge platter was brought out and set before them.

“Is that… Oh wow, is that a swan?”

“Do you eat swan? They are quite good.”

Jennifer shook her head, nervously eyeing the bird in front of her. “I’m not sure if I can eat it. Somehow it seems wrong.”

“What do people eat in…Maryland?”

“Not swan,” she muttered. Then she caught him looking at her and felt her cheeks heat up again. “I’m sure some people eat them. But where I come from, we eat beef, pork, and chicken. We also eat a lot of fruits and vegetables. And don’t even get me started on junk food, soda, and chocolate.”

Edward’s eyes lit up. “I have heard tell of chocolate. Lucy is quite fond of the stuff, as are her sisters. They have not found a way to get it here, but I would not be surprised if they are victorious.”

"I hope I get a chance to meet them."

He took a bite of the bird, and she averted her eyes as he chewed.

"There is much unrest, and I would not have them travel to Somerforth. Mayhap in the autumn."

She was disappointed but understood. Still, she ached to meet others like her. "Is that why there are so many guards everywhere?"

He nodded, his mouth full. Jennifer wasn't used to drinking so much wine, and she felt lightheaded. She was thinking about what she'd seen earlier in the pantry when talk at the table turned to politics and war and someone named Armstrong. After the whole gay fiasco, Jennifer wasn't going to jump to conclusions until she knew something was wrong with what she'd witnessed. After all, maybe Maude and the man were having an affair?

Jennifer caught a glimpse of the redheaded girl as she brought in more wine. She touched Edward's sleeve. "That girl. How long as she been at Somerforth?"

He looked to where she was pointing. "Maude. I took her in as a child. Her family were slaughtered because her father was English and her mother Scottish. We found her curled up in the hay."

"I thought I heard her speaking what I'm guessing was Gaelic?"

"Nay, you must be confused. She has no Gaelic."

She let it drop, deciding it wasn't any of her business

if the girl slept around. They married young here, so who was she to say what was appropriate behavior?

He saw her eyeing the swan, which seem to be eyeing her back. As if he read her mind, the corner of his mouth twitched. Edward reached out and turned the platters around so the swan was no longer looking at her. He met her gaze and grinned.

"Thank you. I know it's silly, but I felt like it was looking at me." He passed her vegetables and bread. "I didn't think you ate many vegetables?"

"My brothers and I eat more than other nobles. We have heard over and over how good they are for you."

It was her turn to grin. She could imagine getting a lecture from a modern-day woman on eating your vegetables. The carrots were in some sort of spicy sauce that had a bit of an aftertaste, but she shrugged it off, hungry as usual, and cleaned her plate, using bread to sop up the last bit of sauce.

After supper, Jennifer felt funny. Then again, she had traveled seven hundred years through time and had to look at a swan all through the meal. It was either lingering time-travel lag or nerves.

The tables were cleared and pushed against the walls, the benches stacked as men vied for the best spots to sleep. The knights slept out in the garrison. It was all very efficient.

Edward was speaking, and she tried to focus on the words but kept shaking her head to clear it. The man kept wavering in and out of focus. Better cut back on the wine tomorrow.

"Mistress, are you unwell?" The alarm on his face made her wonder how awful she looked.

"I don't feel so good. Maybe I should go to bed. I'm sure I'll feel better in the morning."

Edward spoke to one of his men so quietly that she couldn't make out what he said. He took her arm, the heat from him warming the chill spreading through her bones.

"Can you stand?"

She pushed back from the table. "Of course." But when she did, her stomach revolted and her knees turned to jelly. The room spun and Edward's voice sounded far, far away.

The floor was a ways away. She was floating. No, Edward was carrying her again. Jennifer held tight to keep from falling.

"I'm sure I'll be..." She pressed her lips together, afraid to say any more. Saliva pooled in her mouth and she had a hollow feeling in the back of her throat. When Edward took the stairs two at a time, she had to close her eyes. Sensing her distress, he jogged even faster. As they twisted and turned, making their way up the stairs, her stomach rolled like a ship caught in a tropical storm. Any moment now she was going to lose it. Squeezing her eyes closed, Jennifer chanted under her breath.

"Please don't let me throw up on him, please don't let

me throw up on him, please."

Jennifer caught sight of the closed door before Edward shifted her in his arms, lifted a booted foot, and kicked the door open. The man practically tossed her down on the wooden stool.

He knelt in front of her. "Tell me what I may do to ease your pain?"

Her skin was clammy. She swallowed, waiting a moment before she spoke to the Edward on the left.

"Bucket."

Chapter Eighteen

Eyes wide, Edward opened the door and shouted.

Weakly, Jennifer lifted her head. “Edward,” she whispered.

How he heard her she didn’t know, but instantly he was by her side.

“Please don’t. I don’t want anyone to see me like this.”

A knock sounded. He smoothed a hand down her hair. “As you wish.”

“Please, hurry.”

She heard him speaking to one of the guards. The door shut and he was back, thrusting a bucket between her feet.

“There is a guard posted at the door. No one will enter. I will tend you.”

It was no use. She couldn't hold it in any longer. Jennifer leaned forward and out came supper. Mortified to be barfing in front of him, she wanted to scream, but could do nothing. There was no way some servant was going to stand there and watch her puke. If only there was a ladies' room where she could lock herself in a stall until she felt better.

It seemed to go on forever. Jennifer heaved again and felt Edward's hands on her shoulders. A memory surfaced. First year of college and her getting sick after a mean girl had put ipecac in her drink. This felt similar. It wasn't the stomach flu. At first she'd thought food poisoning, but this was so much worse. The stabbing pains made her double over, feeling like she was dying, being ripped in two from the inside. Was it a side effect of traveling through time? She'd ask Edward if any of those other women were sick like this. Or had she messed up history and this was some kind of punishment?

Time ceased to have any meaning. Sometime, what seemed like days or years later, Jennifer managed to sit upright. Sweaty, clammy, and cold all at the same time, she felt like something even the cat wouldn't bother to drag in.

"I'm so sorry. I feel so awful."

"I will send for a girl to help you undress. You will sleep and be well on the morrow."

She grabbed his hand, cringing that hers was wet and

clammy. “Please. Don’t. It’s bad enough you’re seeing me like this. I couldn’t bear for anyone else to see me so sick. I have a hard time being around people I don’t know.” Another pain made her double over. “Just leave me. Aren’t you afraid you’ll get sick?” She knew how much people in this time worried about catching a fever.

He shook his head, the movement making her dizzy.

“Nay. I am never unwell.” He looked like he was about to say more, but gulped then averted his eyes as he asked, “Can you undress yourself?”

Undress? At this point she’d be lucky if she could walk.

“Not a chance.” Jennifer shook her head and winced as the movement made her groan in pain.

Edward’s nostrils flared, but he didn’t say a word. He swept her up again, supporting her weight, holding her as gently as a small child. His hand went to her waist and the belt and pouch hit the floor with a thud. Next came the dress.

Being so close to him, she could feel the tension radiating through him. He paused. “I will make haste. Close your eyes and lift your arms. I will not let you fall.”

Before she could think about it, Jennifer did as he said. He jerked the under-tunic over her head so fast that she didn’t even sway before his arms were encircling her again. But the act of putting her arms up over her head made her stomach revolt and her eyes flew open.

"Bucket," she gritted between her teeth before he bent her over the bucket. The smell of sick permeated the air. Completely disgusted with herself, she could only imagine what he thought. How could she look him in the eye again after this?

When she thought she was empty, she motioned with a hand, and somehow he knew what she meant. He pushed the bucket to the side with his foot and lifted her up, fully supporting her in his arms.

"You will sleep in your chemise."

She didn't have the strength to shake her head. "I can't. It has vomit on the front." A tear ran down her cheek.

While she probably should've been embarrassed, she felt too horrible to care. To give him credit, he didn't bellow at her. Instead he sat her down on the stool.

"Hold on to me." He put her hands around his waist. Then he pulled his tunic over his head and stood there bare-chested. With a look she couldn't interpret, he blew out a breath, the muscles in his neck standing out. Too bad she felt too rotten to ogle him. He should have been carved from marble. Sculptors would weep over his body. The lines were perfect.

"I will do my best not to look upon your form."

She nodded, and he helped her to her feet again as he muttered to himself in Norman French. The French *merde* she recognized, but couldn't find the energy to smile. He was so tense that she was afraid to make any sudden movements.

"Hold my tunic."

She took the shirt, still warm from his body, and held it. With one fluid motion, he pulled the chemise over her head, and somehow she managed to hold on to his tunic.

In a strangled voice he said, "Tunic."

She dropped it into his hand and he roughly pulled it over her head. It came down almost to her knees and smelled of him. Concerned green eyes met hers. "I'm going to carry you to bed. If I needs stop, pound me on the back."

She didn't dare shake her head, so she simply blinked at him. More gently than she thought possible, Edward lifted her up in his arms, his bare chest warm against her thighs. For a moment, she wished she could stay there forever, safe and cocooned within his strength.

He carried her as if she weighed no more than a book or a bag of groceries. And while she was thin, she was by no means some petite thing. It was a novel sensation. So different from the last guy in college she'd dated. The delirium made the memory seem vivid. Real.

The guy had one of those obnoxious muscle cars and the passenger door wouldn't open. Instead of having her climb across the seats, in case she messed up his upholstery, he rolled down the window on the passenger side, hefted her with a grunt, and slid her through the window into the passenger seat.

He was in great shape and loved to spend hours working out at the campus gym, so she would've thought he could've easily lifted her, but apparently not. When he sat in the driver's seat he was all sweaty. Looking her over with a critical eye, he told her she was a hell of a lot heavier than she looked. Jerk. Needless to say, it was the last time she went out with him. So it was a delightful change to feel like she was as light as a feather when Edward didn't change his breathing or grunt.

One of the servants had made the bed from when she'd slept in it the night before. He flung the covers back and carefully laid her down. Edward had started to draw the curtains around the bed when she stopped him.

"Please, leave them open. I don't like to feel closed in."

"I will fetch you drink to rinse out your mouth." He placed the bucket next to the bed on the floor. "In case you have need of it. Lean over and let loose." The corner of his mouth twitched just barely, so slightly that if she had been staring at his face that she would've missed it. When he left, softly shutting the door behind him, mortification swept through her again.

It was bad enough to be sick in front of someone you knew or loved, but to be sick in front of a stranger that you were attracted to even though you didn't want to be? Jennifer wondered if she'd been thrust into the second circle of hell.

As she lay there, the combs from her hairdo poked into her scalp. With an immense amount of effort, she managed to tear the beautiful objects from her hair, scattering them on the floor. Panting, she lay back against the pillows.

Another bout of nausea took hold of her, and, afraid she would miss the bucket from so high up, Jennifer slid off the bed, landing on the floor with a thud. The cool stone felt delicious against her fevered body. She gripped the bucket with both hands and threw up again, wondering how it was possible there was anything left to come up.

She hadn't heard the door open, but there he was. Strong hands held her hair as she heaved out her guts.

When she finished, he put his arms around her to lift her off the floor. A hand on his arm stopped him.

"Leave me."

"You needs be abed."

"I'm afraid I'll be sick again and ruin the sheets."

He scoffed. "You are sick and should be abed. Do not trouble yourself. I will care for you."

And she believed him. There was no reason she should, having only met him a couple of days ago, and yet deep within her soul, Jennifer knew he would take care of her. And in her delirium, she decided that with him by her side, she would live through the night.

The man scooped her up and deposited her in the bed, then pulled the covers up to her chin.

"I'm so embarrassed."

"You are pale as snow. Rinse your mouth out." He handed her a cup of water, but when she sniffed, she found it was cider. She rinsed out her mouth and spat into the bucket. He had replaced the bucket, and there was another sitting by the hearth. Jennifer didn't even want to ask what he had done with the other one.

He stood up to leave, and she made a sound in the back of her throat. Instantly he was by her side. Another tear slipped down her face. "Please. Don't leave me. I'm afraid I'm dying, and if you go, I won't see the sunrise."

He kissed her on the forehead. She heard him speaking to the guard at the door, then he was back, dragging the chair across the floor to the bed.

As her eyes drifted closed, Jennifer felt the warmth of his hand as he stroked her palm. Too spent to speak, she surrendered to the nothingness.

Chapter Nineteen

"Is the lady unwell?" Maude thrust her bosom at Alistair, the guard posted outside the faerie's chamber.

His face was grave. "Aye." He looked down the corridor then whispered, "She may die."

"I will pray for her soul." She was filled with joy. Holding up her basket so he could see inside, she pressed against the man. "I have brought cherries in honey, the lady's most favored dish."

"Nay, she cannot eat." He looked pale in the dim light. "She cannot even drink broth without purging."

"Then I will come back on the morrow." She smiled as she left the castle. The odd woman would no longer watch her.

As she passed through the gates, one of the guards called out, "Where you off to, Maude?"

She waved at the man. "Off to fetch herbs from the water's edge. I won't be long."

"Do not tarry. The gates will close for the night soon."

Once the guard was no longer watching, she ran to the woods. Deep in the wood was a meadow, where she would meet her love.

No one followed her. Maude looked around before calling out, "Are you there, then?"

Hamish Armstrong stepped out from behind a tree, and she ran to him as he gathered her in his arms, kissing her, hands fumbling under her dress. He was older than she by a score, and so handsome, even with the ugly scar the wicked English gave him in battle. Hamish had promised to care for her. He had told her how terrible Lord Somerforth was. Raping and killing the weak. Eating children when none were watching. Maude crossed herself. Aye, Hamish was a good man.

Their lovemaking was over too soon. He smoothed her skirts down and leaned against a tree. "Do they know I was in the castle? Did the wench with black hair tell that bastard Somerforth?"

Maude shook her head. "Nay. She did not. At supper, I made sure she would not tell his lordship what she had seen."

"What have you done?"

"Poison. She is dying. On the morrow she should be dead." She frowned. "I don't know if the poison will work. She should be dead by now, yet she lingers."

He pulled her to him, stroking her hair. "Why not?"

"She's a faerie," Maude whispered.

Hamish looked thoughtful. "The Armstrong could use a powerful faerie. He could take Somerforth with ease if he had a faerie under his power. I will send word and find out what we must do." He idly stroked the scar on his neck. "We will need iron to bind her."

Hamish reached in her dress, fondling her. She pressed against him. "When will we marry?"

He stepped back. "When Lord Somerforth is dead by the Armstrong's blade, I will be free to marry you. Stay in the castle and keep spying. We need you. I need you, love."

He kissed her again, setting her on fire, then melted away into the trees as she looked after him longingly. She would watch the faerie. Aye, she would do anything for the man she loved.

"I want a bath."

Edward did not grin. His lady was in a foul humor, and he did not want another boot thrown at his head. She had been recovering from her illness for a sen'night, and her irascible moods were to be feared.

"Then on this day, you will be pleased." He stood

back, and servants entered carrying a wooden tub. 'Twas not as large as the one in his chamber, but 'twas improper for her to bathe in his chamber until she was his lady.

"Really?" She clasped her hands together. "Oh, thank you, Edward."

As the water heated, he pulled the stool to her bedside. "Shall I read to you?"

"Don't sit too close. I stink."

He sniffed. "Perhaps a bit."

She feigned outrage. "You're supposed to say, no, lady, you are a delicate flower and would never have an odor about your fetching person."

"Your accent is awful. I do not speak thusly."

"Aye, you do."

"Harrumph." He opened the book, some tale to cause womanly weeping about a knight and his lady. Jennifer watched him. Did she find him pleasing? Every day he came to her chamber to pass the hours. They had talked of family and of her world. So many wonders. His brothers' wives had given up the marvels of the future. Might Jennifer stay too? He knew she was opposed to marriage. Her own sire and dam were with others. In her time, men and women grew tired of marriage and simply found another. The church no longer held the power it did now. The men of her time were not men of honor.

The first days, he was filled with dread she would die.

The healer said ’twas the meal, but no others were ill. Edward believed there was trouble afoot. A person wishing his lady ill will. Brom agreed and thought ’twas poison. As of yet, his captain had not found the one responsible.

“My lord?” One of the servants stood before him. “Your lady’s bath is ready.”

“Finally.” Jennifer sat up, swayed, and turned the color of the stars.

“Easy, love.”

He lifted her from the bed. She wore another of his tunics, had refused to wear her clothes until he let her up from the damn bed as she bellowed at him.

“Shall I have them stay and aid you?”

“Please.”

Edward eased her into the bath and nodded to the two women. “I shall be in the lists. When you are finished, dress and I will carry you out to the garden.”

Her eyes shone, and he prayed she would not weep. He could not bear to see a woman weep.

“Promise?”

“Aye, you have my word.” He said no more as she kissed his cheek. “Give them my tunic to wash or I will have to fight with no clothes.”

She scowled. “And have half the village come to stare. Don’t worry, they can have this smelly shirt.”

He heard her sighing as the women bathed her. Thinking of his lady in the bath, being washed, sent desire coursing through him, so he took himself to the lists. Swordplay would distract him from her shapely arse.

Edward wiped his brow. He had run through the garrison, saw to matters requiring his attention, and now he stood back, hands on hips.

"She will be most pleased."

He looked to his friend. "Think you?"

"Aye." Brom fingered the gifts. "How much gold did you give to the abbey?"

"A great deal, but it will be worth every coin to see her smile."

"If you say." Brom looked unsure. "I would give my intended a horse. Practical and useful. No flowers that die, or foolish trinkets."

"A horse?" Edward snorted. "This is why you have that scar above your brow."

"'Twas worth it. She was a fine wench."

Edward rolled his eyes. "I will woo Mistress Jennifer, then I will wed her."

"Better you than me."

Chapter Twenty

Was he ever coming to get her? Jennifer was thrilled to be clean and no longer stinking like week-old garbage. She'd groaned when the women scrubbed her hair. The healer and Edward said it was a bad case of food poisoning, but if it was, why hadn't anyone else gotten sick?

After a while, she'd decided it was a lingering effect of time travel. But wow, she'd never been so sick in her whole life. The first few days, she swore she was going to die.

Not eating anything but broth for a week had made her cranky. She'd been dreaming of pizza, and mac and cheese, and tacos. Not to mention chocolate and her favorite cereal.

Alistair had been a pain in the butt over the past

week. Sure, he was just doing his duty, guarding her. But every time she tried to leave, there he was, outside the door, barring her way. She scowled at him, and for the first time he scowled back.

"You frowned at me."

"Lady? I would not."

A small giggle escaped. "Oh, yes you did. I'm telling Edward."

He looked panicked. "Nay, lady. My lord would be most displeased."

"You're mad you've had to stay inside all week watching over a mere woman, aren't you?"

Alistair clasped his hands together. "'Tis my duty to watch over you."

"Admit it and I won't tell Edward you're being mean to me."

The man looked horrified. He swallowed and looked down the corridor as if another guard might help him, but there was no one. His shoulders slumped.

"Aye, 'tis true."

Jennifer laughed for the first time in a week. She laughed so hard she cried, her side ached, and she started snorting. Pulling herself together, she patted his arm. "I wasn't really going to tell on you. I'm not a rat. I just wanted to hear you admit how horrible it's been to be stuck inside all week."

She'd come to like Alistair. He was eighteen and took his duties very seriously. So much so that she could imagine him outside Buckingham Palace as tourists tried to get him to react to whatever crazy thing they were doing.

He looked relieved. “You should not jest so, lady.”

When she whirled around to go back in the room, a bout of dizziness hit her. Fingers grasped the door but missed. Then strong arms swept her up. She’d know the feel of them anywhere.

“Edward. I was going to come down and find you, but Mr. Crankypants wouldn’t let me pass.”

Alistair blanched at Edward’s look. Too bad she couldn’t see it—she bet it was a doozy.

“I will see you in the lists later.”

The poor guy turned even paler and fled down the corridor. Edward grumbled under his breath as he carried her down the stairs and outside. She waved to a few of the people who’d come to see her while she was sick. The men were in the lists, and she smiled at one of the archers. His aim was atrocious, but he made up for it in gusto.

“Where are we going? I thought I was going to watch you practice your swordplay?”

“Womanly, the lot of them.” He cursed. “Nay, we will spend the afternoon in the rose garden. There is a gift for you.”

“Presents? I love presents.”

He chuckled. They entered the walled garden, the scent of roses permeating the air. The day was warm, the sky blue, and the man she'd fallen hard for over the past week and a half was as perfect as if she'd conjured him up with a magic potion.

In the center of the garden were a fountain and a stone bench.

"Close your eyes."

She did as he asked. Waiting. Then she felt him put her down on the bench, but he didn't sit beside her. There was a rustling before he said, "Open your eyes."

"Oh!" There before her was the most wondrous gift. She reached out, and, knowing what she wanted, Edward stepped into her arms.

Her voice was choked. "It is the best gift I've ever gotten. How can I ever thank you?"

There before her was everything she needed to paint. An easel made of wood and a bundle on the ground unrolled to display the contents. There was a stack of parchment and wood panels for sketching and painting. Assorted brushes, pen and ink, and a beautiful wooden box that was so ornate it looked like a jewelry box.

Edward set it beside her and opened it. "Does it have what you need?"

He sounded unsure. "The monks said 'twas what you would require." He touched a brush. "They are made from squirrel."

Jennifer looked at the tiny jars. Pigments in various colors. She held up each one, opening it and exclaiming over the colors. There were also sticks of mineral pigments: umber, red and yellow ochre, and lime white. When she opened one of the jars, she quickly closed it again and gasped.

"That's ultramarine. It must have been ghastly expensive."

"The monks were delighted to take my gold." He ran a finger down the side of her face, twisting her hair between his fingers. "The color is the same as the dark flecks in your eyes. The moment I saw the color, I knew you must have it."

"Oh, Edward." Tears threatened but didn't fall. "I'm so very happy."

He held up two more jars. "One of the monks said these are for water and egg to make tempera."

"I'll paint the castle and the gardens and the people." She looked at him, feeling shy yet aching. "Would you sit for me?"

He startled. "You wish to paint me?"

"I do."

"Aye, my visage should be captured. The future men in your time are weak and should see what a knight of the realm looks like." The arrogance was back, and she grinned.

"Of course, my lord."

"Harrumph." He pulled her on his lap. "Tell me all you would paint." With a finger, he tilted up her chin. "I would send the monks wagons of gold to see you so pleased."

She laughed. “Don’t say that. You haven’t seen how much I love to paint. We might have to live in a hut after I squander all your gold.”

Chapter Twenty-One

During her stay, Jennifer had managed to avoid getting on a horse. They were pretty, and she'd fed them carrots but ride? No way.

So how was it she found herself nervously eyeing a beautiful black horse with a white patch in the center of its forehead that looked almost like a heart?

Edward came striding toward her. The man pulled all the energy to him, every eye watching him. The movie-star effect.

"The cook packed the tarts you enjoy." He put his arms around her waist, and she wiggled way. "Is aught amiss?"

She took another step back. "No. Why don't we walk to the coast? A nice, long walk would be lovely. It's a beautiful day."

"Do not be foolish. The horses are faster."

But she took another step back. The stable boy stood waiting, and there were a few of Edward's men around. They would all laugh at her.

Up on tiptoe, she whispered in his ear, "I can't ride."

"You recovered a sen'night ago. Are you unwell again?"

"Shhh." She put a finger to her lips. "No. I never learned how."

Edward blinked at her. "You are unable to ride? How do you travel in your time?"

His men, hearing, took a few steps closer.

"Nice. You were supposed to whisper."

He looked abashed. Alistair eyed her as if she were from another planet, which, given the years, wasn't too far off base.

"You are a woman. How have you never been astride a horse? Was your sire cruel? Did he beat you and lock you in your chamber?"

They were drawing a crowd. Everything was closing in, and all she wanted to do was run away. But she'd been pushing herself out of her comfort zone. Trying to get used to being around more people. There wasn't much privacy in medieval England. So she straightened and looked each man in the eye.

"When I was a...child, my sire sent me to learn to ride for a...sen'night. Since then I have never been on a horse. Where I come from, people do not ride horses."

This caused all kinds of discussion.

Edward pressed his lips to her ear, sending shivers down her back. "Cars?"

Not trusting herself to speak, she nodded, but the smug look on his face pushed the shivers away. So she stepped on his foot.

"Cars go much faster than horses."

"Harrumph."

As they stood there grinning at each other as if tied together by an invisible thread, Brom sauntered up, glanced between them, and grinned. He slapped Edward on the arm.

"Haven't seen such a smile since we were at court."

For a moment Edward frowned, then he grinned at her. "A beautiful woman will make all men fools."

Heat traveled up her ribcage. "All beautiful women?"

Brom laughed.

"Nay, mistress. Only you."

"Oh. Well then."

His men looked just as amused, and she'd had enough of being out of her comfort zone for the day.

"Guess you better help me up on this horse."

Edward lifted her up. "Midnight is gentle. She will follow Thor."

Just like she'd follow him wherever he went, but of course she wouldn't tell him that. His head was big enough as it was.

When she was little she used to have her dad tell the

story of meeting her mom. He always said her mother kept multiple men on a string before picking him. That the woman always picked the man, no matter how much the man wanted to think otherwise. Of course, her mom looked like a beauty queen, and still did thanks to an injection or laser here and there, while Jennifer, well, she had good skin and really thick hair. Seeing herself reflected in his eyes was when she honestly felt as beautiful as any movie star or beauty queen. When he looked at her, it was as if no one else existed.

They rode to the coast, a leisurely ride as she told him about painting the blacksmith while he worked.

“Truly? You find such things lovely?”

“Yes. Day-to-day life. The small moments. That’s what I like to capture.” She winked at him. “Don’t worry. I’m saving the best for last.”

Brom snorted. “Do not make him more vain than he already is, mistress.”

“Be silent, dolt.”

Alistair and two other men were with them. A few days ago, one of Edward’s men had found a scout from one of the clans on Thornton lands. Since then they’d been on high alert. Someone had been stirring up both clans, spreading rumors of Edward and his men capturing women and children. The women they supposedly ravished and the children they ate. How anyone could believe such nonsense astounded her, but apparently the storyteller was quite convincing.

It was the end of July, and Jennifer had been thinking of home, trying to decide what to do. On one hand, she wanted to go back and tell everyone what she'd seen, but on the other, she yearned to stay. Ever since Edward had taken care of her when she was so sick, she'd been falling for him. He'd found a way over the walls she'd erected. As time passed, she'd opened herself more and more, believing he was different. To stay here with someone who loved her? Her parents and brother had their own lives, and she had no one else who would really miss her. There had been rain but no terrible storms, so Jennifer hadn't been forced to a decision, but it was only a matter of time. Would he ask her to stay? She peeked at him as they came to a stop. It was nice he wasn't a ladies' man, but when would the dratted man kiss her?

"We eat, then walk along the water."

"Of course, my lord."

He grinned at her, knowing when she called him "my lord," he was being bossy.

"Eat, but beware." The men settled on the ground as the horses grazed. Edward spread out a blanket for them and unpacked a feast.

Right on time, her stomach growled.

"You eat and eat yet you are not round," he said. "Where does the food go?"

His eyes twinkled, so she knew he was teasing. "In my hollow leg."

For a moment he looked stricken, then, seeing her face, he threw back his head and laughed. "'Tis a fine jest."

"I don't know, really. My mother is the same. We eat a lot but never gain weight. But I don't talk about it. Women in my time are obsessed with how they look, and everyone wants to be skinny." She cringed thinking of the mean girls she'd encountered over the years.

"Tell a woman you can eat whatever you want without gaining weight and they might burn you at the stake." She laughed. "Not really, but they might if they thought they could get away with doing such a thing."

Edward stroked his chin. "Women when wronged are as vicious as a cornered beast. Remember what happened to my brother John?"

"Exactly. So I keep quiet."

"You are wise beyond your years."

Chapter Twenty-Two

They ate until they were stuffed. The cherry tarts were Jennifer's favorite. As she licked her fingers, she caught Edward watching her. He took her hand and licked a tiny bit of cherry off her pinky. She wanted to whimper. Normally clear green, his eyes had darkened to the color of winter spruce. Jennifer leaned forward.

A throat cleared, breaking the spell. Edward scowled at Brom, who merely arched a brow. Jennifer wanted to stamp her foot and scream. Damn him and his chivalry. The man had appointed himself or Alistair her chaperone, since she didn't have one. It was beyond annoying.

Edward was grinning at her.

"What?"

"Come. We will walk along the water and I will woo

you away from meddling old women."

"You want to woo me?"

"'Tis what I have been doing."

"Oh."

He intertwined his fingers with hers as he led her down the path and they walked along the cove. The men stayed above, on guard. Jennifer sat on a rock and took off her boots and stockings. Holding up the dress, she waded into the delightful water.

"You have fetching ankles." He was staring at her bare calves. Before, she'd worn shorts and tank tops and never thought twice about it. What would he think seeing her in a bikini? Being covered up all the time made any glimpse of skin tantalizing. When she'd catch him bare-chested after spending a morning in the lists, her mouth would go dry. He'd draw a bucket of water and throw it over his head, and she'd watch as the water ran down his muscles.

"Could we go for a swim?"

He seemed to go pale under his normally tan skin.

"'Tis too cold."

"No, I dipped my toes in—it feels wonderful."

But he didn't move. She took another step, up to her knees.

"Nay, Jennifer. Come out of the water. 'Tis dangerous."

"Don't be silly..." But she saw how stiffly he stood, a look on his face she had never seen. Fear.

She came out of the water, taking his hands in hers. She said quietly, “Edward. What is wrong?”

This incredibly fierce and proud man trembled. When he looked at her, his face was stark.

“The water.”

“Here. Come with me.” She led him over to a low rock. He let her push him down without a word. The rock was small, he was huge, and so she sat next to him, almost in his lap.

“Tell me.”

His gaze went to the water. “When I was a lad, fostering with a lord my sire knew, we took a journey by ship. There was a great storm. The mast broke, water came rushing in, and the ship sank. Men were in the water, sailors, mostly, so they could swim. There were others, knights who could not, and they drowned.”

His hands were cold, and he was gripping her so tightly that she thought he might break the bones in her hand.

“You’re crushing me.”

“Apologies.” He loosened his grip but did not let go, as if she were his personal life raft.

“Then what happened?”

“I saw dark forms in the water. A huge gray fish with many teeth ate a horse, and then the beast came back and ate my lord as he was clinging to pieces of the wreckage.”

Jennifer stroked his hands over and over, pressing

her leg against his. He whispered, "The dark fishes ate many of the men, ripping them to pieces as I watched. I do not know why the fates spared me that day. Ever since, I do not care for the water."

"I'm so very sorry. I can't imagine what it must have been like to survive such a terrible thing."

Edward took a lock of her hair and twisted it through his fingers.

"You believe me about the beasts in the water?"

"They're called sharks. And from what you described, it sounds like a great white shark among the other sharks."

"You have seen such fish?" The color was slowly returning to his face as interest took over.

"Yes. I have seen them in the sea and in a place called an aquarium. It's a building where people pay to go to see different kinds of animals and fish from all over the world."

"And yet you swim?"

She nodded. "I do. The chances of being...attacked or eaten by a shark are something crazy, like one in almost four million. Whereas a person in my time has a one in five chance of dying from heart disease."

"Truly?"

Jennifer nodded. "I swear."

"This heart disease. I have heard Lucy and her sisters talk of disease. What happens to kill a person?"

"When a person's heart stops working suddenly or...

well, let's say there are many things that can happen to a heart, but what I'm saying is, sharks are scary, especially after what you went through." She kissed the knuckle he had smashed during swordplay the day before. "If I had been in a shipwreck and seen people eaten by sharks, I doubt I'd ever get in the water again. Why don't we go back?"

"Nay. You wish to swim. We will go in the water." He swallowed a few times and eyed the calm water as if any moment a great white shark would leap out and eat them, but he straightened his spine and nodded at her.

Somehow she knew she needed to lighten the mood, take his mind off the horrific memory.

"I'm going in. Join me whenever you're ready." She took a step toward the water.

He swallowed. "In your dress?"

"No, in my chemise." And before he could say another word, she'd dropped her belt and pulled the dress and under-tunic over her head.

The man looked absolutely scandalized. Then his look turned predatory. He took off his tunic and boots and, clad only in his hose, lifted her in his arms and waded into the water.

Jennifer couldn't imagine the inner strength it took Edward to get in the water.

"Bloody hell, you should have kept the dress on." He eased her into the water. They were up to their chest. His eyes went to her chest and stayed there a moment.

He swore under his breath before turning and scanning the area.

"This way." He moved until they were sheltered by rocks. He went under and came up slicking his hair back. They swam for a while, and he pulled her against a flat rock. Jennifer could feel the change in the air. As she watched, his hand came out of the water, and he ran his thumb across her lips.

"So beautiful."

She kissed his thumb as he went still. In a flash, he'd pressed her against the rock, pinning her in place with his arms, the wet chemise the only thing separating them. Edward tilted his head down, capturing his mouth and she leaned in to him, twining her arms around his neck, feeling the tenseness of his muscles beneath her skin. His lips were firm as he nudged her mouth open with his tongue, caressing, tasting. She made a sound deep in her throat and pulled him to her, running her hands down the bare skin of his back as his mouth melted against hers.

Chapter Twenty-Three

The ache in her back made Jennifer stretch to work out the kinks. With a critical eye, she stood back from the painting. Over the past week, she'd done a bunch of sketches. The workers in the kitchen were always moving around, and no one had time to sit still for her, so she worked quickly, getting the sketches down so she could paint from them later. Now, she wiped her nose and put a touch of red in the fire on the hearth.

Alistair had become her personal guard and chaperone, and followed her everywhere. Though when she spent a lot of time in one place working on a painting, he drifted a bit away, close enough to hear her yell, but she knew it must be boring to watch her all day.

A woman with a baby came into the kitchen, looking around. She saw Jennifer and stopped. "The guard at the gate told me to wait here."

Jennifer wiped her hands on a cloth and took a step closer. "Your baby is beautiful."

The woman smiled, showing a few missing teeth. "Aye, he's a bonnie lad."

She was Scottish. What was a Scot doing here? With the rising tensions, Jennifer was shocked to see the woman standing in the kitchens as if she had every right to be there.

The woman wasn't really more than a girl, now Jennifer got a good look at her. She saw the woman eyeing the bread.

"Would you like some bread? You must be hungry after your journey."

The woman shook her head, but Jennifer knew the hungry look well. So she pushed the loaf to the woman, along with a small jar of cherry preserves.

"Go ahead. I've had three slices already. The cherry preserves are fantastic."

"Yer not from here."

"No. I'm from far away."

The woman accepted the statement and put the baby on the table while she ate.

"Do you have family here?"

The woman looked up, chewing. When she swallowed, she said, "Nay, I've come for his lordship."

Interesting. While she pondered the girl, Jennifer fetched her a cup of ale.

"I have heard of Lord Somerforth's odd lady. Some say you are a faerie."

Taken aback, Jennifer sat down across from the woman.

"No. I'm not."

The woman shrugged. "Others say you bewitched him." She chuckled. "He's a braw man. I'd fight for him to warm my bed."

Well, what did she say to that?

The woman told Jennifer of how she and the babe would have died without Edward's help. What she said next had Jennifer almost knocking her cup over.

"Wait. Who is the traitor?"

"I dunno. Only that they are here in the castle and meet with kin to the Armstrong to plot to kill Lord Somerforth. I came to warn him, and my debt to him is repaid."

A commotion prevented Jennifer from asking the hundred questions in her head. Especially if this traitor could be the man with the scar or the redheaded kitchen girl. She'd bring it up to Edward when the Scottish woman told him what she knew.

Men carried a man into the kitchen, and it was like someone had prodded an anthill with a stick. People everywhere. They laid the man on the table and Jennifer almost gagged. He had a horrible gash down his thigh and was moaning in pain.

It was one of the men Edward had ridden out with

that morning.

"Where's Edward?"

One of the men looked up. "He is well, lady."

She let out a sigh of relief.

"Is the healer on the way?"

"Aye, lady."

Then she'd get out of the way. Jennifer packed up her supplies and easel, and in the commotion forgot about the woman and baby. When she turned around, they were gone.

Alistair had fashioned a strap so she could carry the easel and satchel holding her box and supplies over one shoulder. She lumbered out of the kitchen and heard voices coming from an alcove near the great hall. Later, she would think back and know it was something about the tone of his voice that stopped her in her tracks.

A couple embraced, the woman kissing the man as if she were drowning. There was a bundle on the woman's back. A baby. When they broke apart, Jennifer thrust her fist in her mouth to keep from crying out. It was the Scottish woman and Edward.

Chapter Twenty-Four

Edward firmly pushed the Johnston woman away as he wiped his mouth. One of the men had told him of her arrival, and when he went to find her, she threw herself at him, kissing him before he knew what was happening. He wanted no other. Only Jennifer. He had spoken with the blacksmith. The man did fine work, and would fashion a wedding band with a rare stone. It cost him dearly, but 'twas worth the gold. The pale blue diamond was the same color as her eyes.

"I thank you for telling me of the traitor." He looked her in the eyes. "If the Johnston will not find you a husband, I will find you an Englishman who will care for you and the babe. But hear me well: I am promised to another."

She reached out to touch his face, and he took her

hand, stopping her.

"You are not betrothed," she said. "I would have heard."

"Nay, not yet, but soon."

"The beautiful woman with hair like night. Some say she has bewitched you."

"She holds my heart. I will not dishonor her." He stepped around the woman. "You owed me no debt, but I am grateful for the information."

The woman didn't meet his gaze. "Aye. I will not come again. The Johnston has a cousin I will accept as husband. Farewell, Lord Somerforth."

"I will send one of my men to see you safely home."

She pulled her hood up. "Nay, I travel alone. 'Tis safer."

"There is a traitor at Somerforth. The Johnston woman confirmed it."

"I have not found out who." Brom watched a wagon leaving the castle. "What of Maude? Her mother was a Scot."

"She has been here her whole life. It cannot be." Edward frowned. "Watch her to be sure."

One of the guards called out, "Riders approach."

A handful of men on horseback galloped into the bailey. He would recognize his brother anywhere.

"Christian. You should have stayed at Winterforth."

His youngest brother dismounted. "Why haven't you visited? Poor Henry. Charlotte is expecting another babe and is in a terrible temper. We received word of your future girl. All the women are in a foul humor since you forbade them to travel to Somerforth."

Embracing his brother, Edward wiped dust from his eye. "There are nefarious schemes afoot. A traitor at Somerforth."

"And your future girl, Mistress Jennifer." Christian looked around. "Where is she?" He touched Edward's sleeve. "Bloody hell, what happened?"

"'Tis naught but a scratch. We were attacked out riding. Johnstons." He clapped Christian on the back. "The lists or a drink?"

Christian paled. "Drink. Then I would meet your woman so I can tell all. Charlotte threatened to chop my head off if I do not tell her everything. Women." He threw up his hands.

"Have you lost another betrothed?"

His brother did not answer as they went inside the hall.

Jennifer spent the afternoon in the rose garden pouting. The man was so busy with his Scottish girlfriend he hadn't even noticed she was missing. As the hours passed, she wallowed and thought of home.

In Baltimore, the city had gotten to her. No matter how many times she went to the harbor to look at the water, it wasn't enough. The crime and ugliness made her want to go to the mountains, paint, and be a hermit.

She'd stayed in school, changing majors, unable to decide what she wanted to be for ages. It was fun learning new things. With so many choices, how could she pick one?

When she tried, she saw all the possibilities stretched out before her and couldn't make a decision. After eight years, her parents had had enough, so she ended up with a degree in art history and no job offers. Her father was disappointed, but her mom...she claimed a migraine and "took to her bed," as she called it. As far as her mother was concerned, the fact Jennifer hadn't graduated with an MRS degree was the worst disappointment of all.

For once she'd evaded Alistair, and now she had no one to send for food or drink. Hungry and thirsty and getting crankier by the minute, Jennifer decided to confront Edward. She'd give him a piece of her mind.

The womanizer. The ass was always stomping about, grumbling and bellowing at everyone. Maybe he had a point there. She tried it. "Wow, this feels great. No wonder he stomps about so much."

She bellowed and tried out a few choice swear words. Yep, it felt bloody great. Stomping into the great hall, she barked at the first servant to cross her path.

"Where is his high and mighty annoying lordship?"

The man blanched. "In the solar with Lord Winterforth."

Figured. The single brother was here. They were probably planning a night of debauchery visiting the village wenches. Why not go on a road trip and kiss every woman in the entire damn country while he was at it?

Grumbling under her breath, she came to the doors of the solar. The door was ajar; she heard voices.

"Aye, Jennifer is a bothersome wench."

How had she been so stupid? Feelings hurt, she turned away and made it halfway down the corridor until she stopped. A servant passed, carrying Edward's sword.

"Where are you going with Edward's blade?"

The man showed her the crack in the emerald. "My lord was fortunate he did not lose his hand."

She needed that sword, so she summoned her best mean-girl voice. "Give it to me. I will take it to the blacksmith. You might drop it, and our lord would be most displeased."

The man took one look at her face and handed over the blade. Pleased with herself, she went to her chamber, wrapped the sword in a cloak, grabbed her easel and satchel, and took one last look around.

She was bothersome? He preferred someone else? Fine. She'd find Connor. It wasn't too far across the border. If she was careful, she'd be okay. He would feel obligated to help her. So she'd stay with him until there was a storm and she could return to her own time, where she could rebuild the walls around her heart. Somehow *he* had snuck up in the deep of night and smashed them to bits, and she hadn't lifted a finger to stop him.

Chapter Twenty-Five

When she made it through the portcullis and halfway to the woods, Jennifer should have known something was up. It shouldn't be that easy, not with the castle on high alert.

"Where are you off to, mistress?" Alistair fell into step beside her, a grin on his face.

She practiced scowling and stomping. "None of your bloody business. Begone." But of course he followed her. Changing course, she walked until she saw the mill. She needed to paint the scene; it was calming and would make the perfect addition to her collection. Alistair stood beside her. What was the use of having a guard if she couldn't order him around?

"Leave me so I can be angry."

The guard backed away from her. Jennifer sat on the

bank, listening to the wheel creak as it went round and round. It was so peaceful that she sat and watched it. Once she calmed down a bit, she'd paint the scene, and then she was leaving to find Connor.

A pretty girl came out.

"Mistress?"

"I wanted to sit here by the water for a while."

The girl disappeared and came back with cups of cider for them both.

"You are the lady from the castle? The one who paints such beautiful paintings?"

"Yes, that's me. Thank you. I thought I'd paint the mill." She looked at the girl. Obviously shy, she didn't meet Jennifer's eyes when she talked. The girl either looked at her feet or off into the distance.

"Will I be in your picture?"

"You will. Would you like that?"

The girl nodded. They sat in silence for a bit until the girl haltingly spoke. Telling Jennifer about her life and how much she enjoyed baking. As the girl talked, Jennifer let the words wash over her until something caught her attention.

"My father says Lord Somerforth will offer for me. I will be a great lady."

"How...nice."

While the girl talked, doubt flooded through Jennifer, and her temper came back with a vengeance. She knew Edward had his lid popped. All the signs were there. He was so ready to be married that he'd wed the next nice girl, no matter who she was. The miller's daughter or her—what difference did it make?

Forget it. He was not the one for her. It was better to be alone. Edward was trouble. Not just with a capital T, but all caps TROUBLE.

No, no, no. No more mooning over the hot English knight. Remember Charlie? How he destroyed her mom? He was husband number two. Her mother spent a month in bed after catching him in the dining room with the housekeeper. On the table. When her mother got out of bed, the first thing she did was sell the table.

"Are you daft, woman?" Edward thundered.

Jennifer heard a squeak. The miller's daughter ran for safety. Too bad Jennifer hadn't sketched the girl or the mill yet. She'd have to rely on memory once she got to Connor's home. If she painted him a picture or two, maybe that would be payment enough for taking her in and hiding her from Edward.

Jumping up, Jennifer turned to see him seated on his horse looking like some ancient bloody warrior come to claim his prize. Not going to work this time.

"Go away and leave me alone." She scooted the bundle closer to her.

The awful man pointed at the tip of the blade sticking out from the cloak. "You are a thief. You took my sword. Why didn't you steal a horse as well?" Edward dismounted and stalked over to her. Jennifer refused to look at him.

“I need the sword. The horse. Well, I didn’t know how to care for him, and I wouldn’t want him to suffer.”

It was quiet except for the turning of the wheel. Where was her guard? She turned to see Alistair trudging back to the castle. She hoped he wouldn’t be in too much trouble for letting her escape.

“Where will you go?”

She didn’t answer.

“You can’t go back. To your home. The sky is blue—there is no cloud and no storm.” He sighed. “Why do you vex me so?”

Eyes narrowed, she stomped until she was an inch from his chest.

“I’m not staying where I’m not wanted. I’ll go to Connor; he’ll help me. I can stay there until a storm comes.”

“He will tumble you in the bloody stables. I forbid it.”

“Forbid? You forbid me? Who in the hell do you think you are to forbid me?” She poked him in the chest. “I think I should be the one forbidding you.”

“Bloody future women. Never listen. Always think they can do what they please with no thought of anyone else.”

“You said I was bothersome.”

“’Twas said with affection.”

“I don’t believe you. You’re a liar.”

He roared at her. Like he was the injured party.

"You insult me, madam."

"Good. Now go away and leave me alone, you womanizing jerk."

"Nay. I will not."

Pacing along the bank, Jennifer called him all kinds of names, using slang to hopefully make him wonder what she was saying. Her fury ruined the peaceful scene.

Edward took hold of her arm. "Enough. You will cease calling me names. You will come home now. And you will obey me."

Oh, hell no. "Obey? Listen here, you egotistical dumbass, you might be some powerful medieval lord, but I'm a modern woman and I do what I want, when I want."

She was so furious that she picked up his sword, pointing it at him.

He held his hands out, moving toward her. "Put down the blade."

Jennifer shook her head. "I hate you." The end of the sword quivered.

The horrible man must have heard something in her voice, as she watched the anger drain out of him.

"Why are you angry with me?"

"The miller's daughter said you're going to marry her. If that wasn't bad enough, I saw you."

He waited. She wanted to hit him. He was going to make her say it.

"Kissing that woman with the baby in the alcove."

For a moment he looked confused. How many women had he been kissing that he wasn't sure which one she meant?

"I have made no offer to the girl's sire. Nor will I." He tapped his lip a moment. "You said kissing?" Then he brightened. "Aye. The Johnston woman."

Her mouth fell open. She dropped his sword and pushed him as hard as she could. Edward stumbled backward, tripped over a clump of grass, and fell into the pond. When he surfaced there was something green on his head. A duck paddled by, quacking at him, and she lost it. No matter how hard she tried, she couldn't hold it in. The laugh bubbled up and spilled out of her mouth. She was laughing so hard, she doubled over, crying.

When the laughs had dwindled to snorts, she wiped her eyes and looked at him. He dumped out a boot and a frog hopped away, which, of course, made her laugh all over again as he scowled at her and put his boots back on.

"I'm still mad at you."

With three strides, he pulled her to him. "She kissed me. I pushed her away and told her my heart belonged to another."

"Oh." Who was it? No, she would not ask. Jennifer tried to pull away, but he held her closer.

"'Tis you, you little fool."

She looked up at him and saw the truth in his face.

“I am a dolt. I should have come to you and told you so you did not hear tales from those who would be jealous.”

“You don’t want the miller’s daughter or the woman who kissed you?”

He sighed. “Nay. A future woman has bewitched me and ruined me for all others.” Water dripped on her face, and he wiped it away. “Forgive me?”

The anger left her. She should have asked him, but she’d jumped to assumptions again. Though this one had merit, given the revolving door of men in her mother’s life.

“Already done.” And then she lost her train of thought as he lifted her up and his lips met hers. He trailed kisses from her cheek down her throat and across her eyelids. She sighed into his mouth, her hands touching his face and hair. As he pressed his mouth to hers, she lost herself in the scent of him and surrendered.

Chapter Twenty-Six

Jennifer had tried to be useful, but it hadn't worked out very well. Edward had plenty of servants to do everything, from cleaning to polishing silver to making candles and doing the laundry. She'd tried to help cook, but it was a disaster.

The look on Edward's face as he ate the pie made her laugh until her side ached. Insisting it was delicious, he finished it, but she'd noticed Brom feeding his portion to the dogs under the table. The captain of the guard had winked at her, and she did the same when Edward wasn't looking.

Then she'd tried embroidery, but as in her own time, she didn't have the patience. It took forever to complete one tiny design. Her work was like the pig who painted with a paintbrush in his mouth, while the rest of the women's skill? They were Monet.

Gardening had also been a fail. Maybe in time she'd come to recognize what was what, but for now, Edward suggested she should paint. The man went on and on, saying how he needed her paintings on his walls and for his brothers. It was kind of him, but made her think: what did the other women like her do in this time? Were they ladies of leisure, or did they have skills?

She at least could work with the cook to decide the menu, but she wasn't yet comfortable approving purchases. Not until she had a better understanding of the cost of things.

So she'd retreated outside to paint. This morning the fog had been thick with a fine mist of rain, making the world around her feel magical as the music from Jennifer's favorite show, *Outlander*, played in her head. Sure, it was set in Scotland and she was in England, but the mood fit. Looking out over the lush green landscape as the fog started to dissipate, she was content. With a critical eye, she looked from her painting of the woods to the woods standing silent.

A growling noise filled the air as her hand went to her stomach. This time it wasn't her, it was Alistair, who turned red when she grinned.

"Sorry I kept you so long. I'm hungry too. Let me finish up and we'll go eat."

Before she ended up here, Jennifer used to pretend she was happier being alone and left to her own devices.

During her time here she'd come to see it was a coping mechanism. A way not to get hurt. After all, if she risked nothing, she had no chance of building lasting connections with others.

She scooped a bit of dirt into an empty jar. It mixed well with water, and she could try using it as paint. The cherries she'd snatched from the larder made a perfect red, while the fresh blackberries she'd found yesterday worked well after she'd smashed them through linen. Wood ash made gray, chalk gave her white, and various flowers gave her bright yellow, orange, red, and pink. Green was the easiest, as she could use grass, mint, or spinach. The carrots were a bit gritty, but after they sat a while they should work relatively well.

Jennifer had annoyed Brom until he told her the cost of the paints. She almost had heart failure, and decided on the spot to make some of her own to experiment with and see if she could save a bit of money. Hard times were ahead, and rich or not, she wanted to pull her own weight in one area.

Edward had read a letter to her from Elizabeth, who was married to his brother Robert. She and the others wanted family portraits and scenes of daily life. Edward promised they would take a long trip next month so she could meet everyone. In anticipation, he'd given her gold for new dresses. One of the girls helped her pick out the fabrics. So far, she hadn't selected a lady's maid. Three of the girls seemed perfect, and she didn't want to hurt anyone's feelings, so she waited, hoping to figure out which one to pick. Then again, Edward told her she could have them all, but it seemed a bit excessive. Six other castles. Each of his brothers and William and James all had their own castles.

Finally a chance to talk to others from her own time. Trade stories, commiserate over the loss of showers, and to find out everything they knew about Edward. Jennifer couldn't wait to go, but she wanted to be back in time for Christmas to spend it at Somerforth. Christmas. It was months away, yet she'd begun to think of this time as the place she truly belonged.

She sniffed the jar of dirt. Jennifer wasn't sure how long her homemade paint concoctions would keep. She needed to make notes. The egg tempera had worked out well once the cook provided her with vinegar. The experimentation was part of the fun. Finished packing up her supplies, she followed Alistair and the men back to the castle.

"I will take your paints to your chamber, lady."

"Thank you, Alistair. Then make sure you eat. I know you get cranky like I do when you haven't eaten."

He blushed. "Aye, lady."

She'd missed dinner. Thankfully, in the kitchen she found a plate with bread, fruit, cheese, and a blackberry tart that cook had saved for her.

After she'd finished the meal and washed it down with a cup of cider, she caught the eye of one of the many kitchen lads.

"Where is Edward?"

"In the lists, lady."

Several of the servants had been horrified when they caught her drinking cider. It was considered lower class. Oh well; she liked it, and it was a nice change from wine or ale. On her way outside, she spoke to a few of the servants. Where was Maude? The girl seemed to know Jennifer was watching her.

She'd told Edward of her suspicions. Brom questioned the girl. The captain knew she was hiding something, but he was not convinced she was the traitor. They'd agreed it must be the mystery man whom the girl pretended not to know. That was fine. Brom could rival any police detective; he'd find out who the man was and where he was hiding.

In the lists, several of the men practiced swordplay, some wrestled, and others were practicing with longbows. The clang of steel drew her attention. There he was. Muscles bunching and flexing as he parried and thrust. If he could come to the future with her, he'd make a fortune training body-conscious men. A body like his couldn't be found in a gym—it required hard work.

Even as a child, she'd loved the ballet, the lines of the body as the dancers moved. It was the same seeing Edward in hose. Why had it ever gone out of fashion?

Sunlight reflected off his hair. He'd pulled it back.

Was that a ribbon? Jennifer clapped a hand over her mouth to keep from giggling. The man had taken her blue ribbon to tie his hair back. How many colors of blonde could she count within the golden strands?

Ever since she'd met her closest friend, Maddie, in first grade, Jennifer had wanted blonde hair. Maddie had perfect spiral curls spun out of gold. Not hair like hers, black as a crow. And straight no matter what. She'd curled it, set it in rollers, even tried a perm once, but nope, it remained thick, heavy, and straight. On the plus side, she never woke up with bedhead.

Jennifer later wondered what clued her in to the impending arrow. Was it the sensation of the air moving, or maybe a shout penetrated her brain? She didn't know as she dove for the ground, barely avoiding the arrow aimed at her face.

"Damnation, you could have killed her." Edward watched helpless as the man turned, the arrow flying toward his lady. He'd never been so happy that Roderick's aim was so bloody awful. "Your aim is supposed to improve with practice, is it not?"

"Apologies, my lord." The man hung his head.

"Go practice in the field where you can't hit anything

but a tree or rock."

The man fled the bailey. Edward couldn't breathe until he held Jennifer in his arms, patting her to assure himself she was unscathed. "Are you unharmed?"

"Truly. I'm fine."

He snorted, relief filling him. "Dolts." She had been outside so much that her skin was turning golden. He wanted to be alone with her, away from meddling women. "Shall we ride? You can gather more blackberries."

"I'd love to." This beautiful woman was his. The blue dress she wore darkened her eyes. He looked closer and grinned. There was yellow paint on her wrist and neck. And was that a spot of green under her chin?

"What?" She narrowed her eyes. "You're staring at me like I have a frog on my head. What?"

"I like when you bellow at me."

She was annoyed. "I do not bellow."

"Aye, you do. 'Tis most pleasing."

His lady glared at him. "You're so weird."

Anna, John's wife, had taught him the word. He knew it meant odd, but in a teasing manner, so he chuckled.

"Alistair and Thomas will accompany us."

He swept her up in front of him on the horse. Once they crossed the drawbridge, he urged the horse to a gallop, knowing she liked to go fast. He was pleased that she was learning to ride. Thomas had been teaching her, but she had not found her faith in the horse yet. In time she would learn.

A quarter of an hour later, Edward cast his gaze to the sky. “We should go back. Have you enough berries?”

His lady emerged from the brush, eating a handful of blackberries, her palms stained purple. Leaning in to kiss her, he tasted the fruit on her lips before she pushed him away.

“You’ll crush them after all the hard work to pick them.”

“You wound me. Choosing fruit over your lord?”

She tapped her lip with a purple finger. “Hmm, let me think.” She poured the rest of the berries into the basket at her feet. “Never. You are far sweeter.”

Before he could kiss her again, he heard shouts. They ran to the horses.

“We ride.”

“You’re not fighting them?”

“Nay, my bloodthirsty wench, there are too many. If I die this day, how can I wed you?”

She went still against him. “You want to wed me?”

“Aye. You are a bothersome wench, stomping and bellowing about, but I find I do not care for sweet words and biddable lasses. I am ruined for all others.”

“Funny. Very funny, Edward.” He heard the joy in her voice. “That’s the nicest thing anyone has ever said to me.”

’Twas enough for him. She would be Lady

Somerforth, and next year, his brothers would come to see the fine son she would give him.

Chapter Twenty-Seven

"Hamish. Where are ye?"

Maude waited behind the icehouse. It was set into the farthest wall of the castle. The steps went down into the earth, where it was cold all the time. Some said it went all the way to the sea. What they did not know was there was a passageway between the wall encircling the castle and the icehouse. That was where her love was hiding.

Every winter, ice and snow were taken into the icehouse and packed with straw to stay frozen until the next winter. She had to make trips every few days during the summer to chip off ice or fetch the food stored within. Maude told Hamish about the passageway. He would hide there, and when 'twas time he would bring the men in, one at a time to hide them in the passageway until they fought and took the castle from Lord Somerforth. She crossed herself.

The wall opened and Hamish came out, taking her in his arms. "Today we almost had the great Lord Somerforth. In a sen'night he will be dead and the Armstrong will reward me. Then I will wed ye, Maude."

She looked into his face, touching the scar he had earned fighting her lord a score of years ago. A man she had come to know was wicked and evil. Hamish had told her so.

"Two of the men are with me. Soon there will be a great battle and I will bring the rest inside the walls. Then when Somerforth's men are weak from fighting, we will strike and take the castle."

Edward had spent the last few days raiding across the Johnston and Armstrong lands. On the last raid he'd lost two men. A day later he received a message two of his men had been captured and were being held on Johnston lands. Two Scots for two of his men. He took three of the garrison guards with him.

"You should not go." Brom had scowled. "Take me with you."

"Watch over Jennifer and Somerforth. I must be there for the exchange."

"'Tis a trap."

"I will not leave my men to suffer. Tell Jennifer after I am gone. The vexing wench worries overmuch."

Why had he not heeded his captain's words? Edward cursed. Brom had been right, and now Edward found himself locked in a ruined tower awaiting hanging. All because of a long-ago grudge.

In all his years he had not feared death, not until now. Until her. If Jennifer could go back, she would be safe in her own time, but if she could not, she would be alone. Nay, Brom would see her safely to his brothers. They would make a good match for her. And he would haunt the man and wait. Somehow finding her in the future. God would not take him so easily.

When the whoreson Johnston hanged his men, Edward swore to repay the Scot tenfold. The soldiers' women and children would be cared for; he would see to it.

It had taken four men to bring Edward down. He groaned as they dragged him down the stairs. His head ached and he saw three of everything. The three bastards on his right had black eyes and broken noses to show for clouting him over the head with tree branches.

Before they left the ruined tower for the scaffold, one of the men pulled a hood over Edward's head and clouted him again.

Edward woke to jeering. Why was he under the scaffolding, not standing above with a noose around his neck?

"Bloody hell."

"Hush, ye wee bastard." Crouched in the darkness was Connor. The Scot showed him the back of his hand and raised his middle finger.

'Twas all Edward could do to keep from laughing at the rude sign.

"This is the last time I save your womanly hide. When next we meet on the field of battle, I will end you. I may be an outlaw, but I am still a Scot and you are the bloody English."

"Till then." Edward respected the man. "I will give you a clean death and say a prayer for you."

Connor snorted. "I should let you hang and wed your woman." He put a finger to his mouth. "'Tis a jest. She is not for me. Future women are troublesome wenches. I would sooner wed a pig."

Edward ignored the insult. "Why is Gilbert not here to hang me himself?"

"The Armstrong had a fire and is trying to save his

store of grain." Connor grinned. "He is the reason there is a price on my head. I have evened the score."

The Scotsman cocked his head, listening. "The man hanging you has been paid well. He will not remove the hood."

The crowd threw rotten vegetables and jeered. Done boasting, the Johnston told his people they were safe. No more children would be taken away and eaten by Edward. He rolled his eyes. Then the trapdoor opened and a man fell through, jerking. 'Twas a while before he went still. Edward felt ill. He could have been the one at the end of a rope.

Edward crossed himself. "Who was he?"

"A thief sentenced to death. I offered him gold for his family." Connor grinned. "Aye, you can repay me and then some. I want two of your finest horses as well as gold."

"Done."

The crowd lost interest and went back to their day. The man would be left as a warning. But on the morrow they would find no body, only a grave. Connor had paid the executioner to burn the man. 'Twas the gravest insult to burn a body. No one would know the truth until they heard Edward lived. His legend would grow.

When night fell, they crept through the village as thunder rumbled. By the time they were deep in the forest on the way back to Somerforth, the rain came down and thunder sounded across the sky. Edward wondered if 'twas the same at Somerforth. Would the storm take Jennifer? Nay, he would not think on it. She would be there, waiting for him.

An hour or so before dawn, they were attacked. One of the Scots had seen the thief's face as he burned and knew 'twas not Edward. During the fight, Connor took an arrow through his hand and went down on one knee.

Lightning flashed, and Connor sliced at the two men in front of him with his dagger as the sky filled with voices. 'Twas the most dreadful sound Edward had ever heard. The Scots, full of fear, turned to run.

"Nay, not this morn." Filled with black rage, he buried his sword to the hilt in the first man's chest. The other threw a dagger, narrowly missing him. With one swing of his blade, Edward almost cleaved the man in two.

Connor screamed, the sound turning Edward cold. Helpless, he watched, full of dread as the Scot faded. 'Twas not possible, yet Edward could see through Connor to the trees behind him.

Connor reached out, his mouth moving, but Edward could not hear the Scot over the voices all around them. Lightning struck Connor, and before Edward's eyes, he vanished.

Trembling, Edward vowed never to let Jennifer go. How had she and the others endured such a thing?

"You can't go when you know it's a trap. You are Lord Somerforth and responsible for everyone. Without you we will be lost."

Jennifer had been so upset when she heard what happened to Edward and Connor that she had done something she wasn't proud of. For the first time in her life, she'd raised her fist to another person. After she calmed down she knew it was an effect of the adrenaline wearing off, but still, she was embarrassed.

It hadn't even fazed the man, and she knew she hadn't hurt him, though he pretended she was very fierce.

"Do you swear the sky was not full of voices?" Edward looked pale. "'Twas a terrible sound, unlike any I have ever heard."

"It must be a little bit different for everyone." She bit her lip. He paced back and forth. They were in his solar, and despite the fire in the hearth, she shivered, wanting to ask but afraid. Edward obviously had the same thought.

"You would brave such madness to make the journey again?"

"I would."

He drew his blade, offering it to her. "I vow to aid

you."

Confused, she accepted the sword. "But the emerald was cracked. This is a sapphire."

Reaching into the pouch at his waist, he came out with the emerald. "I saved it for you." He placed it in her palm. "'Tis yours."

"Do you want me to go?"

At the same time, he said, "Do you wish to stay?"

Tears blurred her vision as Edward told her how intelligent, brave, and beautiful she was.

"There's no storm, but we could try. It's so dangerous here. I worry about you. Would you come with me to my time?"

Edward looked around the solar. "My brothers would see to Somerforth and its people. I would go to be with you."

Relief flooded through her. It was time to go home. Reliable like a mountain. Standing for all time. Edward was the kind of man she could rely on. One who would never run; one who would be there. He'd never fall apart. No, he'd handle business and keep her safe. With his very body as a shield. Taking a deep breath, she nodded.

Down in the hidden chamber, Edward sliced his hand and then hers. He twined their fingers together over the emerald and gripped the sword with the other hand. And they waited. Jennifer thought it should have happened. She didn't feel any different.

"Did we travel to your time?"

"It felt different so I don't think so. Let's go outside to be sure."

Chapter Twenty-Eight

Jennifer was sad and relieved at the same time. They were still in medieval England. It hadn't worked. They both agreed the storm was necessary to make it work. Neither of them discussed trying again.

Every day felt like borrowed time together. Edward planned to retaliate, and yet Jennifer couldn't shake the feeling something bad was coming.

Edward rocked back on his heels. "The walls of Somerforth have never been breached. You will be safe."

Exasperated, she blew out a breath. "But you will be outside the bloody walls. I want you safe too."

Psychologists said when people are born, they are only afraid of two things: loud noises and falling. Jennifer snorted. No wonder falling in love was exciting and terrifying at the same time. It was the equivalent of jumping out of a plane and not knowing if the parachute would open. Why did anyone ever step out of that plane in the first place?

Then again, not jumping was like not allowing yourself to love. A closing off of the innermost you. Giving up on happiness, staying in limbo, not truly living. She was ready to live. Edward had already jumped—she simply had to let go and join him.

A serving boy brought a pitcher of wine, and she poured each of them a goblet. No one had seen Maude since Edward returned from escaping the hangman's noose. All in the castle were on the lookout for the traitor.

This morning cook had noticed food missing. The castle was searched, but no one found the redhead. Jennifer jumped with every noise and shadow, sure the girl was somewhere in the castle, hiding.

As she took a sip, it hit her. All this time her mother was braver than Jennifer had ever been. She jumped, knowing she would hit the ground and shatter into a thousand pieces. But she repacked her parachute and got on the next plane, ready to jump again. Hoping one day the man her mom had given her heart to would be there to catch her.

Deep in her bones, Jennifer knew Edward would catch her. She loved him and was pretty sure he loved her. So why hadn't either of them said the words?

Edward and Brom were going on about strategy

while she studied him. The door to the solar banged open and one of the guards said, “We are under attack. Scots. Bloody lot of them.”

“Alistair.”

The knight stood at attention.

“See Jennifer to her chamber.” He turned to her. “Bolt the door until I return. Alistair will stand guard.”

“Wait.” She went to him, and he swept her up in his arms. “Don’t go.”

“I must. ’Tis my duty.”

“Stay with me.”

Edward plundered her mouth, ignoring the sounds coming from his men. His gravelly voice vibrated against her ear, the words low so only she could hear. “Would you care if I died?”

“Very much.”

“Then I shall take care not to.”

“When we return, I will wed Jennifer. Tell her I love her.”

“You need her like a fish needs the sea.” Brom clapped him on the shoulder. “I will guard your back so you may return to your lady.” Then he grinned. “Shall we go kill these Scots bastards?”

Edward laughed. "We shall."

The Scots came screaming out of the fog. Edward lost himself to battle lust, hearing nothing but metal on metal as the smell of death filled the air. He pushed everything else away as he fought on.

Fog made it hard to tell how much time had passed. Edward carried one of his men to a tree, where he would be out of the battle. A battle cry pierced the fog, and he turned, swinging, the sword an extension of his arm as he cut down man after man. The bodies grew higher and higher and still he fought on.

The blow came from above. Two Scots dropped from the tree and he went down to his knees under the rising tide of men. The Armstrong had grown canny, knowing the only way to have the advantage, to kill, was to take Edward's armor and send all his men at once.

The rain fell, turning the ground red. Mud covered his face, the sword bit into his neck, and Edward fell.

Chapter Twenty-Nine

Jennifer stood on the battlements, shading her eyes from the sun as she frantically counted the men coming back from battle. Where was he? She turned to the knight beside her.

"I don't see Edward. Where is he?"

Hysteria threatened to overflow. No matter how she tried to hold it in, she could not. It was like a bottle of champagne, the pressure on the cork as it eased, then the force made it pop.

The man peered intently at the men below. "I do not see him, my lady. But do not fear; he will return. My lord always returns."

She'd had enough of a scare when word arrived that he had been hanged by the enemy. Instead of standing up here wringing her hands, she ran down the steps, to see what she could do to help and take her mind off him. He would be the last, waiting until all his men were accounted for. She just had to be patient.

The women were ready and waiting with bandages and hot water. Jennifer put on an apron, washed her hands, and met the men at the doors to the hall. Time passed in a blur as she ran back and forth, helping wherever she was needed. One of the men called out as she passed by. "Lady?"

Jennifer knelt beside the man. "Try and drink some ale."

The man took a few sips and coughed.

"'Tis my arm. It pains me."

She looked at his left arm, the gash deep and angry, and her stomach rolled over, twisting and turning in circles in protest. It was an ugly wound. Closing her eyes, she bit the inside of her cheek and took a deep breath. When she opened them, she smiled at the man.

"Better finish the ale. I'll fetch a needle."

Who would've guessed she'd be sitting on the floor of a great hall in medieval England stitching up wounds from a battle? Well, she'd yearned for adventure, and it looked like she'd gotten more than she'd bargained for. Jennifer passed the needle through the flame of a candle then poured whiskey over it.

"'Tis a terrible waste of such fine spirits," the man said, looking longingly at the whiskey dripping on the floor.

She poured him a cup. His mournful expression was exactly what she needed, and Jennifer giggled. "It will keep your arm from becoming...putrid." She thought that was the proper word for infected. She'd cleaned the wound as best she could. It wasn't her first time stitching a wound, but it wasn't any easier. The sound of the needle as it entered the flesh. The man grimaced but didn't utter a sound. And she knew how much it must have hurt.

When one of the women had asked her if she sewed, she never expected to be sewing flesh back together. A snort escaped, and the man looked to her.

"Don't mind me. I was thinking of something from home." How could she tell him she was thinking how much she hated sewing by hand and would do anything she could to use her machine? The picture in her head of a modern sewing machine stitching up men's wounds made her laugh. For the first time in her life, she understood why cops and coroners made such awful jokes when they were on crime scenes—it was the only way to get through the horror.

As she moved from man to man, fetching ale, sewing and bandaging wounds, Jennifer kept looking for Edward to come striding into the hall. He must be seeing to the men, or discussing the battle in his solar. As soon as she could get away, she'd go to his solar and chamber to find him, and scold him for not coming to her first. She'd torture him with the silent treatment tonight for making her worry so much.

A man in the corner was swearing under his breath.

"Brom?"

He blinked at her through bloody hair. There was so much blood in his hair and on the side of his face that she wondered if the armor had done any good. The front of his tunic was drenched.

"I didn't want to be here, but one of the women said she wouldn't feed me. 'Tis naught but a scratch."

The rag she'd dipped in water was useless against so much blood. He rolled his eyes, took the bucket from her, and dumped it over his head. He plucked a bucket from a passing boy and did it again. Water sluiced across the floor as the blood washed off. Thank goodness it was a superficial wound.

He grinned at her. "A mere scratch."

"Head wounds bleed terribly. Are you dizzy?"

"Nay. Leave me be."

Jennifer picked a few small pebbles out of his hair. The wound was already clotting, and he'd be fine after he rested. Wiping the last of the blood from his neck, she bit her lip.

"What's wrong, mistress?"

"I haven't seen Edward anywhere. Where is he?"

"He was bringing Albert back. Has he not returned?" The alarm in Brom's voice ratcheted up the alarm until Jennifer thought she might be having a panic attack.

Her voice was shrill to her ears. "He isn't here. I've

looked everywhere."

Brom motioned one of the knights over. "Where is Edward?"

The man looked around. "He must be in the lists."

"Don't just stand there, dolt. Go and find your lord."

The minutes seemed to stretch into hours as they waited. Brom stood, almost fell over from dizziness, and swore as Jennifer helped him slide down the wall to sit.

"You won't do anyone any good if you fall and smash your head open on the stones."

He grumbled about shrews, but stayed put. Finally the man came back, his face pale. "No one has seen him."

Before she could fall apart, one of the Scots being held for ransom spoke up, spitting out the words.

"Aye, I watched the bastard fall. They ambushed him at once, took his armor, stabbed him hundreds of times, and I laughed as the mighty Lord Somerforth died in the mud like an animal. The one who eats children is dead." He spat on the ground.

The knight that had been looking for Edward struck the man so hard his head snapped back and hit the wall. A ringing sound filled Jennifer's ears and everything went wavy. The noise around her sounded like it was being filtered through cotton balls. She swore a storm raged inside the hall. One moment she could see clearly, and the next, black ink seeped in around the edges, taking over, filling her vision until the only thing she could see was Brom's face. His mouth moved but she couldn't hear the words. It was the last thing she saw.

Chapter Thirty

Opening her eyes, Jennifer saw a cluster of men and women huddled over her. There was a cool cloth on her forehead.

"What happened?" But before anyone could speak, she cried out, "Edward." Frantic, she pointed to the Scot. "He said Edward is dead. I don't believe him. I have to see for myself."

One of Edward's garrison guards frowned. "You cannot. The battlefield is no place for a woman."

She glared up at him. "You just try and stop me."

The man looked to Brom. Edward's captain saw the determination in her face. "Stay. I will go with her."

He only swayed slightly when he stood. "Jennifer, I swear it. We will find him."

It was the first time Brom had ever called her by

name, and it made her worry even more. A cup was thrust into her hand, and she saw one of the girls who worked in the kitchens.

"Drink, mistress. You will need it for what you are about to see."

Hand trembling, Jennifer drained the cup and held it out. "One more."

The girl refilled her cup and she drank again. Taking a deep breath, she squared her shoulders. "Let's find Edward and bring him back."

No way would she believe the Scot. He couldn't be dead, he just couldn't. Edward was larger than life, a legend. Sure, he'd been injured, but he was always fine, always victorious. There was no way the man she had fallen in love with could be dead.

The urge to scream was so strong that Jennifer had to bite her tongue. Did it take finding out he might be dead for her to realize she loved him? No. She could afford to indulge her emotions later; right now she had to find the man she loved.

Outside, there were men everywhere. Some wounded, some prisoners. And the smell. She imagined this was what it must be like to walk through a slaughterhouse. The overwhelming coppery smell filled the air, so strong not even the faraway breeze from the ocean could wash it away. Overlaid on the blood was another scent, one that clung to the back of her throat and made her clear her throat several times. As she tried to place it, Brom leaned down and spoke quietly.

"'Tis fear you smell. In battle, the smell lingers. Fear and death."

Her eyes met his, and she saw there the horrors he had seen during his life. The gruff warrior patted her arm. "Edward is probably drinking a pint with one of the prisoners as he tells the man how much gold he will get for his ransom. I am certain he lost track of the time."

"If that's true, I'll kill him myself." Then she burst into tears, all the emotion and worry spewing out of her. Brom patted her on the back hard enough to make her stumble.

The grassy fields looked red, and she avoided looking at the worst of the carnage. Other women moved among the fallen. Some were crying over their men; others... others were taking clothes, weapons, and other things.

"Anything of use is gathered. 'Tis the way of battle." Brom took her arm, guiding her around two men. Their eyes were open and unseeing. Jennifer shuddered as they passed.

They came to a wagon. Men in kilts were loading their dead. "I thought the Scots that survived were prisoners?"

Brom shook his head. "We took all the prisoners back to the castle. Those you see have come to claim their dead. There will be no more fighting tonight. This is a time of truce. They gather their dead, as do we."

Not looking where she was walking, Jennifer stepped in something that squished. An awful feeling went through her as she heard Brom's sharp intake of breath. She tried not to look at what she had stepped in, but failed. A low moan escaped. It was part of a man. The rest of the scene was too horrible for her mind to process. Brom lifted her up and set her back down on solid ground, but her stomach had had enough, and revolted. She leaned over and threw up. Over and over again until there was nothing left.

When she stood, Brom didn't say a word as he handed her one of the failed handkerchiefs she had embroidered for the men. Her work looked like that of a child compared to what the other women did, but they'd seemed happy for the gifts. He thrust a leather bag into her hand. "Rinse your mouth out and spit it out. Then take a few sips. You'll feel better."

Grateful, she took the bag from him and did as he told her. When she handed it back, he wore a different look on his face. One of respect.

"Everyone vomits after their first battle. You have been through several and have not been sick, not even when you tended the men today. You have done well, Jennifer. Edward would be proud of his lady."

"Thank you." She looked at the soiled handkerchief. "I think I'll wash this before I give it back to you."

He grinned at her, helping to lighten the mood, to banish a small bit of the horror that was all around them.

It was an awful job, but they looked over every inch of the field of battle. Some of the men were on their stomachs, and they had to turn them over to see their faces. So much mutilation and death. Jenifer felt like she was swimming in it. And yet everywhere they looked, there was no sign of Edward.

Red stained her from hand to elbow. The words sounded ripped from her throat. "Where is he? He isn't here."

The haunted look on Brom's face must have matched her own.

"I do not know." He turned and looked back toward Somerforth. "There is one last place we can look."

"Where?"

"'Tis a terrible place. Are you sure you want to come with me?"

"I would face all the demons standing at the entrance to hell to get Edward back. Lead the way."

He blew out a breath, his steps slowing as they came closer to the castle gates.

"Where exactly are we going?"

"The black chamber."

The words made her cringe, though she didn't know why. But if Brom was nervous to enter this chamber, she should be terrified. Jennifer didn't utter another word all the way back to the castle, nor when they passed through the gates. Not until they came to a building she had never noticed before. Turning to meet his eyes, she said, “Please tell me he’s not in there. I can smell the death from here.”

Brom’s shoulders slumped. “We must go in and see.”

Chapter Thirty-One

The small stone building stood alone at the back of the castle, against the wall, as if it could not bear to be close to anything else. The stone was blackened on the front, as if someone had tried to burn it at one time, and there were Latin words above the door, almost completely worn off. Jennifer swallowed, filled with trepidation.

The smell filled her mouth and nose, permeating her skin and hair. The stench unbearable as they walked through the door into the dimly lit chamber.

No effort had been made to adorn the building. It was rough stone on the inside, not at all like the keep. She swallowed again as Brom touched her arm.

"This place has stood since Roman times. 'Twas where they brought their dead. Some say 'tis haunted by the spirits of those who have passed."

"I can't breathe."

"Breathe through your mouth. It will help with the stench."

He took a torch from the wall and held it in front of them so they could see a few feet ahead. A man's voice echoed off the walls. Scratchy like an old record that had been played so many times it had degraded in quality. Back home, her friend, Maddie, had loved vintage records, searching high and low for her favorites, swearing the songs sounded better on vinyl.

The man with the discordant voice turned, and Jennifer stopped. He had frizzy gray hair sticking out all over his head, and wore a black patch over one eye. From the smell about him, he not only drank copious amounts of ale, he also bathed in the stuff.

The man ignored them, turning back to the lumps lying on the floors and on slabs carved into the walls. The lumps were men, yet she had a hard time thinking of them as such.

Holding the handkerchief over her mouth and nose helped a little, but saliva pooled in her mouth and she sent up a plea that she wouldn't throw up. She kept telling herself not to, that it would be disrespectful to the poor men who lay here dying. It was an awful place to spend your last moments on earth.

The man sang some sort of song, telling the men it was time to die. To let go and embrace death. Not to fight it or to call out, but to go quietly into the night and not disturb the others around them.

She gripped Brom's arm so hard her fingers cramped, yet he did not complain. When she looked down, her hand was white as a bowl of milk, the bones standing out. Forcing herself to relax her grip, she went up on her toes to whisper, "Wouldn't it be better for them to die outside, looking up at the sky?"

"Perhaps. This is the way it has always been done. Edward did not change things when he became lord. The man singing—his father did the same, as did his father."

Grim-faced, Brom knelt down and pulled a blanket back. A man with red hair lay there, eyes open and unseeing. The cloying smell of death seemed to have weight as it pressed down on her. She felt it in her shoulders and the top of her head. But she owed it to Edward.

If he were here...there was no way she was letting him die in this place. Not a chance his last moments would be hearing that terrible, sad song and seeing the others around him dying, breathing in death, waiting for the reaper to take him. No. She shook herself. Jennifer would find him if he were here, and she would take him outside, cradle his head in her lap, and let him go as he watched the stars.

So she wiped her eyes and one by one checked the men. Some were dead. Others wounded so horrifically that it was hard for her to tell who they were. So she ripped a piece of her dress and wiped the blood and the muck from their faces so she could see who they were.

Though somehow she knew, even if Edward were covered from head to toe in mud, she would know him. A part of her soul would recognize him.

The man's voice came again. "Let go; go to your final rest. Death awaits you. Let go."

She muffled a sob as a man reached up and grasped her wrist. There was a bucket and ladle nearby. She gave him water. As his eyes met hers, his mouth moved, but no words came out. And then he was gone. It was as if one moment there was a living, breathing human being behind his eyes, and the next they were empty. Like glass eyes in animals mounted on the wall. Nothing there.

She ran her hand down his face, closing his eyes, as she had seen Brom do. The smell was getting worse. Dark and cloying, choking the breath from her.

Brom was on the other side of the room. If he found Edward, she knew he would call out. The stone cavern continued underground. Cold air seeped into the room, stealing the warmth from her bones. The black chamber was much larger than it looked from the outside. So many had been wounded.

As she came to the wall, she turned around in a circle, frantic. He was not here. Before she could call out, Brom was beside her. He spoke in a low voice.

"Bloody hell, he's not here, lady. Mayhap the

Armstrong took him and will ransom him."

But a small sound deep in her heart, or maybe it was her soul, called out, and Jennifer turned. She had that feeling in her stomach. Right before cresting the first hill on a rollercoaster. The moment and time suspended until she was falling, falling, falling.

There, behind what might've been an altar at one time, was a bundle of bloodied blankets. She almost dismissed it, when something moved.

"Damn rats." Brom went to kick the bundle, and Jennifer gasped.

Blood thundered in her ears louder than her heartbeat. She stopped him with a hand, trembling. On her knees, she snatched back the sodden blanket. There was a man there. So covered with blood it was difficult to tell what color his hair was. But it did not matter; she would know him anywhere. His tunic was crimson, as were his skin and hair. The beautiful blonde turned burgundy.

"It's Edward." Tears streamed down her face as she touched his cheek. "Edward, please wake up. Don't die."

Brom sprinted out of the chamber, and before she knew it, he returned with three men. "Lady, you must let us take him."

Somehow she found the strength to stand and move back so they could move him.

One of the men retched, and another wept. "Our lord is dead."

Light from above filled Jennifer. "Do not say such things. He is not dead. He will live. I forbid him to die."

The men carried him outside into the setting sun, and she wanted to scream. How dare the sun streak the sky with such beauty when he was dying? It should be gloomy and thundering. Pouring down rain. She turned around and took one final look at the black chamber.

"Please. Let him live. I would give my own life for his."

Chapter Thirty-Two

Jennifer was glad Edward's captain took control. She couldn't seem to make any decision, no matter how small.

Brom barked out orders as the men carried Edward into the great hall, servants scurrying to and fro to carry out his bidding. By the time they carried Edward up to the chamber, the bed had been stripped, and what looked like old sheets had been laid down for when the awful part was done.

His men reverently laid him on a makeshift table, like some pagan offering to the gods. Lying there, he looked even worse than he had in the dark and terrifying black chamber. A few of the women had tears running down their faces as they went about their work. The men either let the tears run freely or quickly wiped them away when no one was looking.

The healer had been seeing to a lad who dropped an axe on his toe. Jennifer looked around the chamber, full to bursting, and scowled. “Leave.” All of the men except Brom and Alistair left the room. No way was she going anywhere.

“I will send word...once we know,” Brom called out as the knights left.

Hot water and clean rags waited. The shaking Jennifer had felt from the moment she stepped into the hall had given way to cold clarity. Time seemed suspended, as if the stars above were holding their breath to see if he would live. The healer grasped her wrist, her grip strong for a woman who looked to be in her seventies.

“Be strong for your man. Brom will aid me in removing his clothes.”

The healer turned away to the makeshift tray she had set up. There were various threads and needles, along with jars waiting to be put to use. The sound of fabric ripping filled the space as Brom cut away Edward’s clothes.

He met her eyes. "’Tis not proper for you to see Edward unclothed.”

The ridiculous comment was exactly what she needed to rein in her emotions. “You tell me when you’re uncovering the good bit and I’ll turn my back.”

A half-smile crossed his face. As she helped cut away

his tunic, pieces of it came away shredded and sopping wet.

"I don't understand. I watched him ride out. He was covered in plate and mail armor. How could this have happened?"

He had so many wounds that it looked like a hundred men had hacked at him with swords. It was a wonder he was still breathing. Alistair had left and returned while they were helping the healer. He blanched seeing Edward's ravaged body.

"You heard the Scot. If so many came against him, in time he would fall. Then they could take his armor and do...this." Brom looked stricken.

Alistair looked like he was going to cry. "Another prisoner said Edward came to and fought back without his armor until he no longer had the strength to fight." He wiped his eyes. "The damned Scots left his armor and sword."

"I will examine the prisoners after." Brom nodded. "Guard the door."

Jennifer ran a finger over a piece of cloth. It was silk.

Brom looked ill. "When the arrow goes in, the head will not pierce the silk, and can be pulled out without leaving the head behind."

She swallowed and blinked but did not cry. There was no time for tears. She had to be strong. For him. Cutting away the last of his tunic, she looked to see Brom had covered Edward's groin with cloth before he called for Alistair.

"Help me turn him over."

Edward groaned as they turned him.

"Are you hurting him?"

"Nay. He is senseless," the healer said. She pointed to a steaming bowl of water and a pile of rags. "Clean off the blood and muck, then I will stitch the wounds."

Jennifer blew out a breath and did as she was told. In the modern world, unless someone was a nurse or a doctor or worked in some other trauma field, the average person didn't see wounds like these. Then again, most modern doctors probably didn't either. They would have seen gunshot or knife wounds, but not so many sword wounds.

She gasped at a particularly nasty wound, swearing she glimpsed bone in his shoulder. Her stomach clenched and threatened to turn over, but she forced it down with an iron will.

Finally she and Brom had cleaned all the blood off, but she'd lost count of the number of wounds Edward had sustained. So many times, she'd stopped, leaned over him, and pressed her face close to his nose to check if he was still breathing. Each time a tiny bit of breath tickled her cheek and she exhaled, sending up thanks he was still alive.

Brom frowned at Edward's side. There was a wound with a piece of wood flush to the skin. He swore viciously. While she watched, he took a piece of cloth from the water and tied it to the stick.

"Mistress?"

The healer mumbled as she looked at the wound. "Aye, push it all the way through." Then she turned to Jennifer. "If ye have a weak stomach, best leave now."

"No, I'm staying."

"Talk to him, Jennifer." Brom touched her hand. He nodded to Alistair. "Hold him firm."

She watched as they pushed the cloth through. Edward screamed and thrashed. Alistair and Brom could not hold him alone. Three more men came in and held him as they finished the grueling task. They were all sweating and pale when it was done.

"That's the most horrific thing I've ever seen." Jennifer bent over, breathing in and out until she was sure she wouldn't pass out or throw up.

The healer put a gentle hand on Jennifer's cheek. "Sit down, child, before you fall over." The woman nodded to Brom. "Hold him still so he does not thrash while he is senseless."

"Yes, mistress."

"Send a girl to fetch more bandages, food, and wine."

Alistair left the room.

With a few moments to wait, Jennifer slid down the wall and rested her elbows on her knees. It was as if the afternoon and evening had caught up to her all at once. Exhaustion weighed down her limbs, her arm so heavy she couldn't lift it to push the strands of hair out of her face. From where she was sitting, she could watch the healer. Brom looked as tired as she, as she noted the strain around his eyes.

When the healer stitched Edward's wounds, she had to look away. It was different than when she'd helped his men—this was him. A cup was thrust into her hands.

"Drink, lady."

Grateful, she drank the wine as she sat there numbly. Her cup was refilled and a platter placed on the floor beside her. Jennifer didn't know what was on it, she just ate what was put in front of her, staring blankly into space.

At some point someone must have taken the cup and plate. Stiff and chilled, she rubbed her eyes. A hush had fallen over the room, the air holding its breath. Brom was sitting next to her, a cup tilted haphazardly in his hands, an empty plate on the floor beside him.

The healer stretched and packed away her things. "I have done all I can. The rest is up to the fates."

Chapter Thirty-Three

Before the healer could leave, Jennifer forced her legs to move. For a moment, she wobbled then gained her balance.

"You'll be back tomorrow?"

The woman's eyes were wise and sad. "I gave him herbs, poultices, and stitched him up to please you and his captain. But it will not matter. Edward has seen his last sunrise and will be dead by nightfall. His wounds are too grievous. Even the great Lord Somerforth cannot thwart death when he comes a calling."

"No. He'll get better like he always does, right?"

The woman took Jennifer's hand in hers, the skin soft and velvety.

"He has not regained his senses. The fever will come and it will take him. The wounds are only part of the danger. There is nothing more I can do. I have made a brew of herbs. 'Tis simmering over the fire. Pour a bit down his throat every few hours. There is nothing left to us but to hope. The fates have already decided his fate—they will cut his life thread."

Brom looked like he'd aged ten years. "I will send for a messenger. We must get word to his brothers."

Jennifer would not let him. It would be like giving in. "No. I refuse to believe he's going to die. Send for the messenger if you must, but do not send the message," she pleaded. "Not yet. You said yourself: it's been too dangerous to travel. Why put his brothers at risk traveling here if he's going to live?"

"They should be here when he passes."

"I am here. And I will not let him die."

Brom was full of sorrow; it radiated out of him and seemed to hover above him, a bluish-gray cloud. "As you wish, Mistress Jennifer. We will discuss it again tomorrow." He paused in the doorway. "You will not leave?"

"Not until we know."

"Then I will have a bath prepared and a clean dress sent for you."

"Thank you."

The resignation in his voice made hers break. "Don't give up on him."

The deepest part of the night passed, and Jennifer managed to get a tiny bit of the healer's liquid into

Edward. She'd always thought of the deep night as the time when death came.

"You can't have him," she whispered. Every time she looked at Edward, Jennifer would imagine standing over him, a sword of light in her hands as she fought off death.

He was so pale and lifeless. She wished she could give him some of her strength. The servants entered the chamber, somber, carrying buckets of water, and proceeded to prepare the bath.

She knew what was happening, but it was as if she blinked once when they'd come in the chamber, and when she blinked again, the bath was steaming, waiting.

"Lady? Shall we bathe you?"

"What?"

"We will bathe you, lady."

Normally she bathed herself, but the out-of-body feeling was so strong that she had the feeling she would slip under the water, drown, and not even notice. "I think this time I would like you to bathe me."

The girls were efficient, undressing her and helping her into the tub. One of them eyed the gown critically. "I do not think we will be able to clean this."

"I could never wear it again anyway. Make rags out of it."

The girl nodded and put it in a pile with the other bloodied rags. They scrubbed her clean as the water turned crimson. At least this tub was large. It had been made especially for Edward. It wasn't like the bathing barrel she had used when she'd first arrived. That tub had a padded seat, and your knees almost came up to your chin. In the copper tub, she could stretch out and let the blissfully hot water ease the tension. The heat and stress made her sleepy.

The scent of roses filled the air as they scrubbed her skin and washed her hair. There was a moment Jennifer swore she could smell blood and the awful stench from the black chamber again. It passed, and she drank deeply of the chilled wine they poured for her.

The girls helped her out of the tub and briskly dried her off as she swayed back and forth. They dressed her just as efficiently, though she could have been wearing a sack and wouldn't have noticed—her eyes never strayed from Edward. Watching his chest slowly move up and down, straining as she looked for any sign he was coming around.

Jennifer sat on the stool while one of the girls combed her hair and the other one tidied up the chamber. She knew they were as worried as she, but none of them spoke of Edward. It was as if by not speaking of what had happened, they could pretend it wasn't real. That he was simply sleeping and would wake any moment.

"I'll fetch food to break your fast."

"Thank you both for all you've done."

She sat next to Edward, dipping cloths into icy water

and laying them across his forehead. Tending him through the fear that constantly waited to take hold of her. Alistair forced her to eat, taking over and ordering the servants to fetch more ice from the icehouse.

Brom came in many times to see if Edward had woken. And to beg her to sleep, but she couldn't. Jennifer tried to explain.

"I can't sleep. If I do, I'm afraid...afraid he will die and I won't know. We cannot leave him alone, not even to sleep. Not after he was in that horrid place."

Brom nodded. "As he is senseless, it will be appropriate for you to sleep in his chamber."

Jennifer croaked out a laugh. "You're worried about propriety and I'm worried about him dying."

Brom's mouth twitched. "Aye. If anything could tempt Edward to wake, it would be the thought of his lady sleeping in his chamber. You should sleep on the floor."

"I'm not going to sleep on the floor. I'm going to crawl in bed and sleep next to him." Jennifer smiled.

The look on Brom's face almost made her happy.

"You cannot."

"I don't think he's going to ravish me today." And then the reality of what she was facing came crashing down around her like waves breaking on the rocks. "I love him and I never told him."

"We all have events in our life that affect us, mold us into the people we are. Do not fault yourself. Edward loves you. He told me. If anyone could tempt death to leave and go back to the underworld, I think 'tis you."

Brom took her hand and placed it in Edward's. He looked at Edward. "If I were God looking down from above and saw the love you have for him, surely I would be merciful and bring him back to you, lady."

When he met her gaze, tears streamed down the big man's face. Jennifer felt wetness on her own cheeks, tasted salt on her lips.

"I hope you are right."

He sniffed and gathered himself. "There is a man on guard. I have sent Alistair to sleep. Call out if you need anything."

As the day passed, supper came and went, and the household quieted, settling down for the night. How could they sleep when Edward was...like this? Because death was a normal part of their lives. Well, she didn't want it to be a part of her life. Before her hand touched his forehead, she could feel the heat radiating off him. His fever was spiking. First he sweated, then he shivered as she pulled blankets on and off him, speaking softly to him. Begging him to come back to her. To stay.

She was long past tired, and yet she could not sleep. Jennifer climbed into the bed, careful not to jostle him. He moaned and called out but did not wake, caught firmly in the grip of the fever.

She pressed her body close to him, willing her life force into him.

"From the moment I got here, you have put others before yourself. Always looking out for your people. You are brave and strong and I have thought only of myself. Being here with you has brought out the best in me. I'm only sorry I didn't get a chance to tell you how much I love you."

Jennifer wiped her eyes, sniffling into her sleeve.

"Please don't leave me, Edward. I don't want to go back. I want to stay here with you. You're not stuffy—you're responsible and steady, someone I can rely on. Don't go...I need you."

At some point her body must have shut down, sleep claiming her, for when she woke the servants had already been in the chamber, built up the fire, and brought more cold water and food and drink for her.

Brom entered as a girl was brushing Jennifer's hair, putting it up in a ponytail. They'd accepted her odd hairstyle without a word.

"How is he?"

Tears welled up, but she refused to let them fall. She met his gaze head-on.

"He lives, but I don't know how much longer he will with such a high fever. Is there anything else we can try?"

One of the servants cleared her throat. "In the village where I grew up there was a man with such a fever as my lord." The girl chewed her lip as she thought. "I don't know what they did, but whatever it was, the man lived.

I will ask my mam."

Jennifer felt like the sun came out of the clouds and shone down on her. "Would you? Would you do it now?"

The girl looked to Brom, who nodded. She hurried out of the chamber.

"Do not give yourself false hope, Jennifer. We must be ready."

"I didn't come all this way just so he could die."

Chapter Thirty-Four

Jennifer had not set foot out of Edward's chamber since they found him, though she did open the shutters for the fresh air. No matter how she tried to explain that fresh air was good for someone who was sick, they wouldn't hear it. The servants were horrified, and finally she gave up, bellowing at them to cease. No wonder Edward stomped about all the time.

Time stretched for endless hours, and other times it moved fast, like a raft bumping down whitewater rapids. She'd lost track of what day it was. When she woke, she thought it might be afternoon. Edward was moaning, thrashing back and forth, and she was afraid he was going to hurt himself. Jennifer ran to the door and flung it open.

"He's going to rip open his stitches."

The knight shouted down the corridor, and three of Edward's men came to hold him down. One of them got a black eye and another a broken nose before he stopped lashing out. They had tried to keep her away from him, but he was still muttering and moaning, unconscious. Jennifer pushed under one of the men's arms, leaned in, and spoke softly to Edward.

"My love. Listen to the sound of my voice. I am here. I vow I will not let death take you. But you must calm, or you will hurt yourself. And you've hurt your men."

Slowly he stopped fighting, and the muttering faded away. Two of his wounds were bleeding again.

"Send for the healer. She needs to restitch his wounds."

As the men left, she heard them talking. The one with long brown hair said, "I'd come back from the very gates of hell if I saw such an angel taking care of me."

The other nodded. "Were I death, I too would pass by and let him live. Let us pray death is a tender bastard."

While she waited for the healer, she blotted his wounds and wiped his brow, kissing the scars covering his body, sending hope into each one.

"Please give him back to me. Even if he doesn't love me, just let him live." Jennifer looked out the window at the sunset.

The door opened and the healer bustled in clicking her tongue. Fast and efficient, she restitched his wounds, forcing more of the awful brew down his throat.

“He is stubborn to have lasted so long. Prepare yourself, child—he is growing weaker and will not last much longer.”

“I’m stubborn too, and if I can hold his spirit here by the force of my will then that is what I will do.”

“We will see, lady. We will see.” The healer looked as if she were about to say something else, but she patted Jennifer on the cheek and left.

Brom entered the chamber early in the morning. “We will take him to the lake. The girl says cold water is what is needed.”

“The lake? What about the icehouse?”

“Nay, the water must flow over his body.” The healer had come back with the girl.

"’Tis a last resort. The cold water will either kill him or it will break the fever. ’Tis the only thing left to do.”

Jennifer looked down at Edward. His cheeks were sunken and there was a grayish tint to his skin. As much as she protested, even she knew it wouldn’t be long. Edward would die if his fever didn’t break. She took a deep breath.

"Then we must try."

Four men carried Edward out of the chamber, bringing back memories of when they'd carried his battered body into the room. Jennifer stumbled, and would have fallen had Alistair not caught her.

"Thank you."

The men took him through the hall. Jennifer caught up to Brom and the healer. "Where I grew up, my mother said salt water was always good for cuts. Can we put him in the sea?"

The healer shook her head. "This time of year 'tis not cold enough. There is a stream nearby. The water flows from deep within the mountain and 'tis always freezing. That is where we will take him."

Filled with despair that this might be the last time Edward drew breath, Jennifer pulled one of the boys aside. "Take two lads with you. Go to the sea and fill your buckets with seawater. I want to wash our lord's wounds with it to help him heal."

Jennifer tapped Brom on the arm. "Could you send one of the men to go with them? I want to put salt water on his wounds."

The captain flinched. "I have been wounded and thrown into the sea during a brawl. It will pain him greatly."

"I'm afraid at this point there's nothing left to lose. I would rather cause him pain than always wonder if it might have helped him."

He didn't argue, instead calling for one of the men to go with the boys.

The wagon brought them close to the stream, and the men carried him the rest of the way. Jennifer knelt down, sticking her hand in the water, gasping at the cold that sliced through her. When she looked up it was to see the inhabitants from the castle. They were lining up along the bank on both sides, hands clasped and heads bowed.

Tears ran down her face as she saw the emotion on everyone's faces. At least today the weather matched her mood. The skies were gray and dull and it was raining.

"'Tis an ancient cure. Many do not survive the cold water. But if this does not kill him, it will break the fever." The healer nodded and the men gently placed Edward in the water, submerging him until only his face was above the surface. He immediately thrashed and cried out.

She stepped forward to go to him, knowing of his fear. Brom placed a hand on her arm and spoke softly into her ear.

"You must let him be. All of his people are watching, and he would not wish to appear weak before them."

As much as it pained her, she nodded, her heart breaking at the pain he was feeling. Edward swore, and from the looks on Brom's and the other soldier's faces, she was grateful he was yelling in Norman French so the rest of his people would not understand most of his words. Several of the soldiers crossed themselves. Jennifer didn't want whatever he was yelling translated.

Finally, when she thought she couldn't stand another minute, they removed Edward from the cold water and wrapped him tightly in wool. The journey back seemed longer.

Back inside the chamber, the healer insisted Jennifer take a bath to warm her. Her dress was heavy from the rain. For a moment she felt awful—she'd ruined two dresses in the space of a week. Somehow, after her bath, she choked down supper. Eyes heavy, she climbed into bed, clad only in her chemise, and pressed her body against him, offering him her warmth. Rain lashed the castle, lulling her to sleep.

The warmth on her face made Jennifer feel like she was sitting outside under the summer sun. Blinking, she sat up. The sun streamed in through the window. It took a minute to realize what was wrong. The bed was empty.

Frantic, she looked around, ready to scream when she saw Edward slumped in a chair, looking pale and tired, watching her.

"Edward. You're alive."

Chapter Thirty-Five

"Edward. How did you get out of bed? You're too weak." His woman leapt from the bed, clad only in her chemise, and kissed his face, his cheeks, his hands.

"If it was not for you, I would be dead." He sighed, remembering. "So many dreams, but through them all I saw your face, heard your voice calling me back to the light."

The woman he loved enough to defy death wept. "I love you, Jennifer Wilson."

Her eyes leaked, the tears dripping onto his chin. "Oh Edward, I love you too. Don't ever scare me like that again."

"As you wish." He pulled her to him, wincing from the pain. "I fear I'm weak as a newborn babe."

"Let's get you back to bed."

He didn't know how to repay her. In the mist, when his enemies came for him, 'twas her voice he heard, guiding him home. The few steps to the bed seemed interminable. Edward wanted to complain, but did not have the breath to utter a word.

She helped him into bed, tucking the covers around him as if he were a wee lad. "I should be in the lists. The men will have gone to fat."

"Whatever you say. I will send for bread and ale."

"Nay. Bring me a proper meal."

His woman put her hands on her hips. He recognized the look, not only on her face, but on the faces of his brothers' wives. She was getting ready to, as the future girls said, let him have it.

"You will eat a small bit of bread. You haven't had anything else in days, and if I feed you a full meal now you'll throw it up. And I am not cleaning up after you."

He settled back against the pillows, enjoying her fussing over him.

"As you say."

She left the chamber, bellowing at his men. He heard a disturbance in the corridor. Brom strode across the chamber.

"I cannot believe you're alive. You must be too stubborn for death to take."

"Has she gone?"

Brom nodded.

"Tell me. What of Armstrong?"

"I fear he is planning another attack."

"Then I must get out of bed. Prepare to fight."

His captain, the man who feared no woman, looked to the door.

"Nay. Your lady will put me to the sword herself. You are still too weak." He backed away out of Edward's reach. "I know. You are the most feared warrior in the realm, but Edward..." Brom's voice broke. "I saw death waiting beside you. Only your lady kept him from taking you."

"Then leave me like an old woman to sleep. But I want to be kept apprised of the situation."

"I will return after you sup."

When Jennifer returned, he accepted the meager bit of food without grumbling.

Mayhap he grumbled a bit.

"You will stay in bed?"

"As you command me, lady."

She sniffed at her person. "I stink. Do you mind if I have a bath?"

The thought of her bathing in his chamber sent a bolt of pleasure through him. If he had his way, they would bathe together.

"Go. Take your bath."

Jennifer clapped her hands and summoned the bath. She did not smell. To him she smelled of the sun, the flowers, and the trees. But he knew women were particular, and he wanted her to be happy. After she bathed, he would ask her to be his wife. She was destined to stay with him. And he thought perchance she was no longer afraid of marriage, for she had not bolted when he told her he loved her.

When the servants put up the screen to shield the bathing tub, his face fell. He had been hoping to catch a glimpse of her as she climbed into the bath, but he supposed there would be time enough for him to look upon her form when they were wed.

He heard her softly humming to herself. Then a splash and she was silent. “Jennifer?”

No answer. Had she fallen and banged her head? Was she drowning? Edward found the strength to push himself out of bed. He landed on the floor with a thud.

“Bloody hell.”

He only tilted a bit as he stumbled across the floor. When he reached for the screen, he stumbled, knocked it aside, and fell again.

“Edward.”

She was wrapped in linen, her skin wet and smelling of roses. “What are you doing? Why on earth are you out of bed?”

“I thought you had drowned.”

She turned a fetching shade of pink all over. “I saw a mouse. I’m afraid of mice.”

Then she realized something was wrong, and looked down, tugging the cloth over her breasts.

“You shouldn’t be looking at me.” She wrapped the

cloth more tightly around her. But it only went to mid-thigh, and he had a long look at her shapely legs and arms. She was beautifully formed. He wanted to trail kisses from her toes to her head.

"Damn it, Edward. You're bleeding all over the floor."

He scoffed. "'Tis nothing."

"Let me help you to bed." He let her pull him across the chamber. By the time they reached the bed, he was panting as if he'd been fighting for days.

She caught him staring at her again. "Turn your head so I can dress."

Grudgingly, he did as she asked. The rustle of fabric made his mouth go dry. When she touched his cheek, he opened his eyes to see her dressed, her eyes bright.

She brushed her lips over his. He wanted to curse. His body wanted to claim her, though he had not the strength.

He saw her lips twitch. "Don't speak."

"What? I wasn't going to say anything."

He scowled at her. "If you fed me a proper meal, I would not be as weak as a babe and could properly ravish you."

Jennifer arched a brow. "Is the ravishing before or after you've spent the day in the lists?"

"Vexing woman."

She simply smiled at him as his heart filled with joy.

Chapter Thirty-Six

A week of listening to Edward grumble and fuss had made Jennifer cranky. He was a terrible patient. Then again, she had been bossy and irritable when she had food poisoning, and he hadn't complained.

Things had quieted down, and she'd finally begun to relax and believe Gilbert Armstrong had given up. At least for now. There was a knock at the door, and she got up to answer. In the corridor, the guard was nowhere to be found. She shrugged. He was most likely in the garderobe. Sitting on the stone was the pitcher of wine and two goblets she'd asked for.

"Jennifer?"

She brought the wine in, shutting the door behind her. "Wine?"

Edward rubbed the sleep from his eyes. He hadn't

shaved in days and looked like a sexy pirate, making her insides clench.

Another knock sounded. "Stay here." She rose to answer it. Alistair was out of breath and sweating.

"What's wrong?"

"One of the kitchen lads saw Maude."

"Send the men to search the passageways again," Edward yelled from the bed.

The guard grinned at her. "He is well?"

"He—" The sound of the metal goblet hitting the floor followed by a thud sent fear coursing through her veins. Alistair pushed past her and cried out, "My lady."

Edward was curled up in a fetal position, groaning. "Eels in my belly."

She reached for the goblet and Alistair knocked her hand away. "Let me." He picked up the goblet and sniffed. "Poison. I fear 'tis the same that was used on you when you...arrived."

It was too much. She'd gotten him back only to lose him again. The floor rose up to meet her face.

Jennifer woke to find herself in bed next to Edward. He grunted and rolled over. She must have fainted. There was a bucket by the bed, and a stack of cloth and basin of water as well. The healer had been here. The scent of her herbs lingered in the air. Jennifer picked up a cup and sniffed. Opium. Edward would be out cold for a while, then. Sliding out of bed, her feet hit the floor. She waited a moment, then opened the door, expecting to see one of the guards. The corridor was empty.

After she'd used the garderobe, she'd go find out what was happening and see if they'd found Maude yet.

Jennifer came out of the tiny room off Edward's chamber to find her way blocked by the very girl everyone was looking for.

"You. You poisoned Edward."

"Aye. You too, witch. When ye first came to Somerforth, I thought you were a faerie, but you're nobody."

The girl's face contorted, and she came at Jennifer with a knife in her hand. As they struggled, Jennifer tried to remember everything Edward and his men had taught her. She yanked hard on the girl's hair, pleased to hear her yelp in pain. Jennifer landed another blow, this one to the side of the girl's face. She jumped back, screaming in Gaelic. Then, realizing Jennifer wasn't reacting, she switched to English.

"Hamish told me how Lord Somerforth eats the children of Scots. You do too."

The girl was unhinged. Jennifer didn't mean to laugh, but it came out anyway. "That is the most ridiculous thing I've ever heard. Wise up. Hamish is using you."

The girl shook her head, a wild look in her eyes. "He loves me. When your man falls, he will marry me."

Maude lunged at her, and they went down, rolling across the floor, struggling for the knife. What happened next seemed to blur into one awful moment. Somehow, Jennifer got hold of the girl's wrist and twisted, pushing with all her might until the knife went in at the hollow of Maude's throat. Unprepared for the amount of blood, Jennifer scrabbled back until she felt the wall.

Eyes open and unseeing, the girl lay there. It was sheer dumb luck Jennifer had killed her. The shaking started in her fingers, traveled up her arms, and ended in her chest. She had killed a living, breathing person.

"I've never killed anyone before." Her teeth chattered and she was cold all over. Edward had found her on the floor and gathered her in his arms. No matter what he did, she couldn't get warm. Somehow he'd heard her cry out and woken from his opium-induced slumber to come to her.

He held her arms, forcing her to look at him. "You

are a brave warrior. You did what needs be done. I would be proud to fight alongside you, my lady."

"How do you live with it? The knowledge you have taken another's life?"

He didn't make light of her question. Instead she watched his face turn grim as he thought. It seemed a long time passed before he answered.

"When you take life during battle, 'tis different than taking life out of anger." He had climbed into bed and pulled her onto his lap, stroking her hair. She relaxed, slowly letting the sensations wash over her.

"Killing because you are protecting those you are responsible for, the ones you love, your home, or your lands, is the warrior's responsibility. Those deaths are forgiven by the church. Maude would have killed us both if you did not kill her." He kissed her neck, and she smelled mint on his breath. They both chewed the leaves after meals if they hadn't brushed their teeth. Gently, he pressed his lips to her cheeks, her eyes, and across her mouth. Light kisses, meant to soothe and heal.

"The taking of life is why women are not made for battle. To bring forth life is sacred. Thus the taking of life is more difficult for a woman because of this sacred duty they carry. 'Tis a great gift to bring life into the world."

Edward kissed each of her fingers. "I know in your time you said women fight for their country. So much change, but the ability women have to create life is why death affects you more strongly."

Since Jennifer didn't have children, at least not yet, she wasn't sure if he was right, but it made sense to her. "Am I going to have nightmares?"

"I will not tell you lies. You will. But in time they will fade. When my time comes to pass to the next life, I know I will see the faces of all I have killed. But I also know I have done so with honor and have nothing to fear from my maker. And neither do you."

Somehow his words washed away the worry. While Jennifer knew it might only be temporary, she would take whatever reprieve she could get. She gripped his tunic tightly and tilted her head up to meet his lips. It wasn't a delicate kiss—it was demanding, yearning for something she couldn't quite articulate.

He knew what she needed and violently crushed his mouth to hers. Heat poured through him into her very soul, warming her for the first time. The ugliness around them faded away as his kisses burned through her body, destroying the death, ugliness, and worry. Replacing them with light and happiness.

Chapter Thirty-Seven

While Jennifer and Edward dealt with the aftermath of Maude's death, Brom had discovered the hidden passageway behind the icehouse and caught not only Hamish but Gilbert unaware. She knew Edward was disappointed he hadn't struck the killing blow, but he bore the news well enough when Brom presented the severed heads at Edward's feet.

She still couldn't believe Gilbert Armstrong had caused so much death, all because he blamed Edward for his only son's death. Edward and Brom had told her that the boy died in battle, a warrior's death, but the news broke something in Gilbert, and he'd been after Edward all these years.

Hamish hated Edward from the scar he gave him when he was a lad in his first battle. Then he'd spread the rumors about Edward eating children to stir up hatred.

Thank goodness it was all over.

The blacksmith presented Edward with the sword.

"'Tis wondrous. It will make a fine gift for my lady."

The man bowed. "I am pleased."

Thunder sounded across the sky and Edward went in search of his lady. She was in the rose garden painting, a streak of pink across her cheek.

"A storm is coming."

"I heard it. I'm just finishing up."

He looked to the darkening sky and saw lightning light up the heavens. Edward took the easel and satchel from her.

"What do you have there, a new sword?"

He held it up. "A gift for you, lady. 'Tis time you had your own blade."

Jennifer clapped her hands. "Let me see." She accepted the sword from him, holding it up. "It isn't heavy like yours."

"Nay, 'twas made for you."

Lightning filled the sky again. "We should go inside."

But she did not move. The wind blew her hair across

her face.

"Jennifer, is aught amiss? Do you not like the blade? I will have another made."

She touched the stone, ran her finger down the hilt and across the edge of the blade before he could stop her. Three drops of blood fell to the earth.

"Edward. I was so very wrong. All this time I thought it was your sword. The emerald."

Over the thunder and wind, 'twas hard to hear. He pulled her toward the keep as the rain fell.

"When I cut my palm, I was holding another stone in my hand. I fell, skinned my palm, and bled on the stone, but when I fell I must have dropped it, and I forgot all about it." She met his gaze, but something was very wrong. She was there but was not.

"It was a ruby."

Lightning arced and she faded as Edward lunged for her.

"She belongs to me. I defied death to come back to her. You will not take her from me." He bellowed to the heavens until his voice failed him.

Edward came to, looking around the room. He had lost her.

"Jennifer."

He heard footsteps. The door opened and there she was.

"I had to use the garderobe. Stop shouting, you'll have half the castle here."

"What happened? The last thing I remember was watching you fade...like Connor."

"You fainted."

He scoffed. "I do not faint. Women faint."

She looked properly chastised, and he decided to ignore her chin quivering. Surely she was not laughing at him?

"Of course, my lord. You are much too fearsome to faint."

"Harrumph. Come and sit with me." His heart ached, for he knew he had almost lost her back to her own time.

"You stayed."

She took his hands in hers. "I saw my old life. And I knew I could go back, but if I did, we would never find each other again, in this life or the next."

A tear fell from her eye. "I saw you in the mist. You were holding on to me. I turned and saw a land covered in blood and tears. Then I saw the anguish on your face as you watched Somerforth and all who live here fall. I took your hand and pulled." She reached out and touched his face, her fingers making him burn to possess her.

"I should not have stolen you from time. I could not let you go. We belong together. Always and forever." He had to wipe a bit of dust from his eye and clear his throat before he could tell her the rest.

"I think what we saw was what would come to pass if we were not together. Or if I had gone forward to your time."

He would not wait another day. "Marry me, Jennifer Wilson. Let this be our first night together as betrothed. We will spend the rest of our days together. What say you?"

He watched her eyes leak. The sound of weeping filled the room, and it took him a moment to know she was happy, not full of sorrow. She wrapped her arms around him, pressing her lips to his, gently then more urgently as he held her so tightly he was afraid he would break her.

"Yes. Yes, I will marry you. I love you."

"And I you. 'Tis only with you I am truly whole."

Books by Cynthia Luhrs

Listed in the correct reading order

THRILLERS

There Was A Little Girl

When She Was Good

TIME TRAVEL SERIES

A Knight to Remember

Knight Moves

Lonely is the Knight

Merriweather Sisters Medieval Time Travel Romance Boxed Set Books 1-3

Darkest Knight

Forever Knight

First Knight

Thornton Brothers Medieval Time Travel Romance Boxed Set Books 1-3

Last Knight

The Merriweather Sisters and Thornton Brothers Medieval Time Travel Romance Boxed Set Series Books 1-7

COMING 2017 - 2018

Beyond Time

Falling Through Time

Lost in Time

My One and Only Knight

A Moonlit Knight

A Knight in Tarnished Armor

THE SHADOW WALKER GHOST SERIES

Lost in Shadow

Desired by Shadow

Iced in Shadow

Reborn in Shadow

Born in Shadow

Embraced by Shadow

The Shadow Walkers Books 1-3

The Shadow Walkers Books 4-6

Entire Shadow Walkers Boxed Set Books 1-6

A JIG THE PIG ADVENTURE

(Children's Picture Books)

Beware the Woods

I am NOT a Chicken!

August 2016 – December 2017 My Favorite Things Journal & Coloring Book for Book Lovers

Want More?

Thank you for reading my book. Reviews help other readers find books. I welcome all reviews, whether positive or negative and love to hear from my readers. To find out when there's a new book release, please visit my website http://cluhrs.com/ and sign up for my newsletter. Please like my page on Facebook. http://www.facebook.com/cynthialuhrsauthor
Without you dear readers, none of this would be possible.

P.S. Prefer another form of social media? You'll find links to all my social media sites on my website.

Thank you!

About the Author

Cynthia Luhrs writes time travel because she hasn't found a way (yet) to transport herself to medieval England where she's certain a knight in slightly tarnished armor is waiting for her arrival. She traveled a great deal and now resides in the colonies with three tiger cats who like to disrupt her writing by sitting on the keyboard. She is overly fond of shoes, sloths, and tea.

Also by Cynthia: There Was a Little Girl and the Shadow Walker Ghost Series.